INVERCLYDE LIBRARIES

			G 2012
1 9 JUL 2012			
2 2 SEP 20	D0590585		2012
1 MAR 2013			

Inverclyde Libraries

34106 002334196

About Leah Ashton

An unashamed fan of all things happily-ever-after, Leah Ashton has been a lifelong reader of romance. Writing came a little bit later—although in hindsight she's been dreaming up stories for as long as she can remember. Sadly, the most popular boy in school never did suddenly fall head over heels in love with her...

Now she lives in Perth, Western Australia, with her own real-life hero, two gorgeous dogs and the world's smartest cat. By day she works in IT-land; by night she considers herself incredibly lucky to be writing the type of books she loves to read, and to have the opportunity to share her own characters' happy-ever-afters with readers.

You can visit Leah at **www.leah-ashton.com**

This is Leah Ashton's fabulous first book for Mills & Boon® Riva™

If you love *A Girl Less Ordinary*,
and want to read more of Leah's writing,
then look for her New Voices 2010 winning entry,
Secrets and Speed Dating, published as part of the
Mills & Boon Loves… anthology, available now!

A Girl Less Ordinary

Leah Ashton

INVERCLYDE LIBRARIES

All the characters in this book have no existence outside the imagination
of the author, and have no relation whatsoever to anyone bearing the
same name or names. They are not even distantly inspired by any
individual known or unknown to the author, and all the incidents are
pure invention.

All Rights Reserved including the right of reproduction in whole or
in part in any form. This edition is published by arrangement with
Harlequin Enterprises II BV/S.à.r.l. The text of this publication or
any part thereof may not be reproduced or transmitted in any form
or by any means, electronic or mechanical, including photocopying,
recording, storage in an information retrieval system, or otherwise,
without the written permission of the publisher.

® and TM are trademarks owned and used by the trademark owner
and/or its licensee. Trademarks marked with ® are registered with the
United Kingdom Patent Office and/or the Office for Harmonisation in
the Internal Market and in other countries.

First published in Great Britain 2012
by Mills & Boon, an imprint of Harlequin (UK) Limited,
Eton House, 18-24 Paradise Road, Richmond, Surrey TW9 1SR

© Leah Ashton 2012

ISBN: 978 0 263 22744 4

Harlequin (UK) policy is to use papers that are natural, renewable
and recyclable products and made from wood grown in sustainable
forests. The logging and manufacturing process conform to the
legal environmental regulations of the country of origin.

Printed and bound in Great Britain
by CPI Antony Rowe, Chippenham, Wiltshire

Also by Leah Ashton

Secrets and Speed Dating*

*Published as part of the
Mills & Boon Loves... anthology

**Did you know this is also available as an eBook?
Visit www.millsandboon.co.uk**

PROLOGUE

Fremantle, Western Australia.
Thirteen years ago

NOT EVEN AS she stood outside Jake Donner's bedroom window, watching the flimsy and slightly askew aluminium blinds smack rhythmically against the glass in the gentle breeze, did Eleanor Cartwright—even for a moment—have second thoughts.

Which wasn't to say she wasn't nervous. Of course she was. Declarations of love, she imagined, were always at least slightly nerve-racking.

But tonight, nerves didn't matter.

She had to do this.

You should tell him, honey. Love shouldn't be kept secret.

She hadn't paid much attention to her mum when she'd said that a couple of months ago. She thought maybe she'd even laughed?

I don't love him, Mum, don't be stupid. We're just friends.

And her mum had done that annoying thing where she raised her eyebrows as if she were the all-knowing, and gently shook her head. It had made Eleanor feel about twelve, not sixteen.

Whatever, mum. He's leaving anyway. There's no point.

And maybe there still wasn't.

But the pointlessness—or not—didn't matter any more.

Since exactly twenty-nine days ago, a lot of stuff didn't matter any more.

Eleanor took a deep breath. She could do this.

Letting Jake leave Fremantle—and her—without knowing how she felt was no longer an option.

A larger pre-dawn gust of air made Eleanor shiver, and it slipped through the opening in Jake's window to make the blinds rattle loudly.

No sound came from his room. Which wasn't all that surprising, given it was about three o'clock in the morning. Plus, Jake slept like a log.

She stepped closer, the dew that coated the long, unmown grass around his house damp against her legs. Jake's bed was right below the window, so, on tiptoe, she slid it open. The window—and the house—were old, and it gave its usual shriek of protest.

'Jake?' she said, hoping the sound had woken him.

No such luck.

So she continued with her plan, gripping the edges of the window, and hoisting herself upwards. Then she would perch on the window sill, reach for Jake, and gently shake him awake.

This, however, was not what happened.

Instead, her momentum propelled her upwards—and inwards—not at all in the way she'd imagined. In the cacophony of the blinds, her own surprised yelp, and then Jake's much louder shout, she found herself bounced from the bed and onto the floor, Jake's body pressed against hers from chest, to hip, to toes. Her glasses had parted ways with her face, but even so Jake's confusion was apparent even in the—slightly fuzzy—moonlight.

'What the hell? Eleanor?'

She nodded, temporarily incapable of speech for two reasons: the impact of hitting the worn carpet, and the realisation that Jake was only wearing boxer shorts.

But then he was up, and away from her, the overhead light coming on a second later. She stared at the naked bulb, doing her best to breathe and think at the same time.

'Eleanor,' he said, 'why are you here?'

He crossed to her, reaching out and pulling her to her feet.

He met her gaze with confusion. 'Why are you still in your uniform?'

She looked down, taking in her crumpled white shirt and knee-length tartan skirt. She'd barely registered what she was wearing. That day, the week—the past month—it had all been a blur.

'I couldn't sleep.'

'So you decided to jump in my window?'

Eleanor just looked at him.

Jake sighed, and he scratched at his belly absently. That belly had changed a *lot* since their many trips to the beach last summer. Now it was firmer, leaner—she could see the angular jut of his hipbones just above where his boxers hung low on his body.

Following her gaze, he hooked a finger in the waistband and tugged them a little higher. But he didn't look embarrassed.

He never did.

In contrast, Eleanor usually felt like a walking bundle of self-consciousness.

His dark hair was a mess, but he still looked really, really great.

Eleanor knew she didn't look great. But at least she'd washed away the evening's worth of dried tears on her cheeks. Besides, her mum had always told her that it didn't matter what she looked like. It was what was inside that counted.

'I wanted to talk to you,' she said softly.

Jake's gaze darted away. 'About your mum?'

'No,' she said. And did he look—relieved?

In the almost month since her mum had forgotten to look before stepping out onto a busy Fremantle street, Eleanor had barely seen Jake.

That had been her choice—hadn't it? For the first few days she'd left the house for nothing but the funeral—the oblivion of sleep the only relief from the indescribable pain of loss.

And then, finally, when she'd returned to school, it'd been alone. Jake's final year exams were already over and so, for the first time in four years, she'd walked to and from school without him.

She hadn't wanted company. Not even Jake.

But now she did. Now she needed him.

And yet he was shifting his weight from foot to foot—like an Olympic runner settling into his starting blocks, mere milliseconds from sprinting away.

No. That couldn't be right. Jake had always been there for her.

She needed to sit, so she did, perching on the edge of his bed. Amongst the bunched-up fabric she found her glasses, and she put them on with hands that shook just slightly.

He eyed her warily.

This wasn't at all how she'd expected this would go.

'I wanted to talk to you before you left.'

'I don't fly out until Monday, Eleanor. That's two perfectly good days you had to come knock on my door at a time I wasn't—you know—sleeping.'

She narrowed her eyes. 'I didn't think you'd mind.'

But obviously, he did.

Just three weeks ago he'd held her hand at the cemetery, his pockets stuffed full of tissues for her—and now he couldn't even look at her?

Jake crossed his arms. Not exactly the body language of someone open to a declaration of love.

Not that it was going to stop her. She'd come this far. Jake acting strange didn't make a difference.

She understood strange, anyway. She could barely remember what it felt to feel normal—to feel like herself. All she had was little pinpricks of the normal and familiar amongst a near blackout of grief.

And this thing with Jake—well, she wasn't stupid. She'd seen the way he looked at her sometimes. She wasn't imagining it. Something *had* changed. She was sure of it.

Maybe she just needed a different plan of attack.

She shot across the room before her nerves got hold of her. Jake's eyes widened as she came closer, but he didn't move.

A ruler length away from him, she stopped, and had to tilt her head upwards to meet his eyes.

She considered reaching out to touch him. The popular girls

at school made it look so easy—they'd absently hook an arm over their boyfriend-of-the-moment's shoulder at lunchtime, or wrap themselves around him at the bus stop.

But she wasn't one of those girls. And she didn't know what to do.

Frustration made her talk quickly. 'I love you.'

It ended up being more a mumble, but that Jake heard every word was obvious in the way his body jerked away from her.

Not the reaction she was after. The churning in her stomach stopped dead.

'No, you don't,' he said. As if that were a fact.

'Yes,' she said, more clearly this time. 'I do.'

He shook his head. 'You're just confused because…'

'Of my mum? No. I knew before. It was her idea I tell you.'

Now he walked away, just a few paces. He turned his back to her, resting his hands on a desk covered in keyboards and hard drives and floppy disks—and a lot of stuff Eleanor couldn't possibly name.

At the back of her mind, she had the feeling she should be crying. But instead, she felt oddly still. Calm.

She needed to walk away, straight across to the fence that separated their houses, then through the three-paling-wide gap they'd used to cross back and forth for years. Back to her room. Tomorrow morning she could come back here, pretend she hadn't meant it, and things could go back to normal.

But Jake was about to leave. Things were never going to be normal again.

'I think,' she said, her heart pounding, 'that you might love me, too.'

This made him spin around, and suddenly he was right in front of her. Crowding her.

'You need to go, Eleanor. Your dad will be worried.'

No, he wouldn't. Her dad wouldn't notice if she stripped naked and ran laps down at Port Beach.

Jake was so close.

She liked the width of his shoulders, and his chest, too. Some of the pretty girls had noticed, but Jake hadn't been interested.

And she'd been glad—really glad—when he'd shut them down. Actually, he'd laid his geek act on pretty thick—thick enough that, if anything, his *weirdo* label had been even more firmly reapplied, which was of course exactly what he'd wanted.

The guy standing right in front of her now, in his bedroom, with his shirt off, was definitely *not* a weirdo in her book.

He was her best friend. The guy who made her laugh, and helped her with maths—which she hated—and that she helped with his English—which he hated. They were a team.

She loved him. And she needed to know if he loved her.

'Eleanor—please, you need to—'

But before he got the words out, she kissed him.

Or at least, she tried to. But by the time she stood on tiptoes, closed her eyes and leant forward—her lips only collided with his cheek.

His cheek.

And it was this—*this*—that finally kick-started what should've been her immediate reaction. People who loved you did not respond with 'no, you don't'.

They definitely didn't turn away from your kisses.

For a moment, the icy horror of humiliation froze her. Froze her with her lips still whisper close to his skin.

'No. I can't do this. I—'

What was he saying? Eleanor could barely hear him, overcome by her own voice in her head.

Stupid. Stupid. Stupid.

How could she have really believed that Jake could love her? Why? Why on earth *would* he?

She wasn't pretty. She wasn't super smart like him.

She didn't wear the right clothes like the popular girls. She didn't know how to flirt, or to kiss a guy. Obviously.

She had to go. She should never have come.

Without a word she stepped around him, climbed onto his bed and halfway out of the window before she registered he hadn't said a word.

Wow. She'd actually thought he'd tell her to stop. To stay.

She looked over her shoulder as her legs dangled outside, her skirt all rucked up around her waist—but she didn't care. As if Jake would even notice.

Jake was watching her. His gaze was full of...what?

Regret?

No. Now she was just being delusional. She knew what it was. Pity. Definitely.

And she had no interest in staying around for that.

So she jumped to the ground, and walked—even though she badly wanted to run—back to her house. Without a backward glance.

Later, as she stared at her ceiling, incapable of any more tears, she managed to unearth one single positive out of the whole horrible mess.

This was another one of her mum's ideas—the absolute belief that something good could be found in absolutely anything. She was pretty sure even her mum would've been stumped as far as finding a positive in having her ripped away from Eleanor far too soon—but this thing with Jake? Yes—there was a positive.

She'd never have to see him again.

CHAPTER ONE

Sydney, New South Wales
Today

I<small>T WAS AN</small> ambush. Plain and simple.

Jake Donner knew it. Every one of the board members who currently watched him with matching unreadable expressions knew it, too.

How long had this been planned? Hours? Days? Weeks?

'No.'

Jake figured that was pretty much all that needed to be said.

'There's no other option, Jake.' This came from Cynthia George, a silver-haired, retired chief executive of one of Australia's major banks who now spent her spare time on a handful of corporate boards across Sydney. As she studied him with what could only be described as a steely expression, Jake was reminded why he was so keen to appoint her to this board.

Intimidating just began to cover it. Pretty damn scary was closer.

But still, he shrugged. 'Find another one.'

Jake forced his body to fall back into the soft leather of his high-backed chair, attempting a fair facsimile of casual nonchalance. But his muscles were tense, and he found himself fighting the instinct to leap up and pace around the edge of the Armada Software boardroom.

This was *not* representative of his usual board meeting experience. *Usually,* the time was spent paying careful attention during the topics that interested him, zoning out during those that didn't, and occasionally congratulating himself on his decision a few years back to extract himself from this excruciatingly boring world of the business he'd founded. Now he had a twenty-eight per cent share of the company, an up-and-coming CEO—also currently studying him across the streaky marri surface of the boardroom table—and a board made up of Sydney's corporate elite—nearly all financially invested in Armada. All this added up to the perfect excuse to pay as minimal attention as possible to the day-to-day operations of the company and instead let the experts worry about it while he did what he was actually good at: coding software.

Up until about a minute ago, this arrangement had been operating flawlessly.

Across the table, the chief financial officer pushed a paper-clipped sheaf of papers in his direction, the pages fanning out slightly as they slowed to a stop.

'Here's an option, Jake. We reduce our FTE by twenty per cent.'

Full-time employees. In an organisation of over two thousand in this skyscraper alone, that was a heck of a lot of people.

'Cutting staff is a last resort.'

The CFO nodded. 'Agreed.' He gestured at the LCD screen at the head of the table and the final presentation slide it still displayed. 'Hence the board's proposal.'

Jake didn't even bother to look at the figures and multi-coloured graphs before him. He was familiar with them all. He might slouch about in his chair and say very little at these meetings, but he read every single board document in detail.

Sales were down. Costs were up. Australia might have weathered the Global Financial Crisis better than most of the world, but Armada had not emerged unscathed.

The facts were inarguable.

But the proposed solution?

Definitely worth arguing about.

'I'm confident that the release of Armada's first smart phone will significantly increase revenue,' Jake said, and he was. Just not as confident as he'd been last night when he'd absorbed the surprising financial report. He'd expected the board to have a typically brilliant solution to what he'd been sure was a temporary problem. But their unease was unsettling. Their solution impossible.

Jake Donner—as the new face of Armada? Nope. Wasn't going to happen.

'There's no need for something so drastic,' he said.

Cynthia smiled without humour. 'A few TV and radio appearances, a conference keynote address and a couple of interviews is hardly drastic, Jake. Armada needs a public face, and you're it.'

He shook his head. 'For a decade the quality of our products has spoken for itself. I seriously doubt wheeling out some computer geek is going to help anything.'

She snorted, an incongruous sound in the perfectly silent room. 'Computer geek? Try infamous multimillionaire recluse. Number two in *Headline* magazine's list of Australia's most intriguing people. Number *one* in *Lipstick*'s most eligible bachelors. The increased publicity for the new phone will be immeasurable should you be the face of the product.'

Jake sank even further into his chair, stretching his long jean-clad legs out beneath the table. He didn't ask to be featured in those stupid glossy magazines. Didn't ask to forever be annoying his long-suffering local constabulary in order to despatch the more than occasional misguided journalist or photographer who trespassed onto his Blue Mountains acreage home.

It was all nonsense. Absolute rubbish. There was no story to be found. No scoop.

Was it *really* that unusual to despise Sydney's concrete jungle? To equate wearing a suit, unending meetings and patently false schmoozing to something only a few degrees south of selling his soul?

Apparently so.

Who cared that he'd rather work remotely from the comfy couch in his lounge room? Who cared that he'd rather stick pins in his eyes than attend some society function chock-full of Sydney's self-satisfied, Botoxed elite? Who cared that he truly believed his private life was private and that a flat no-interview policy made his life significantly easier?

Well, according to the ten sets of eyes focused on him right this second, and the substantial business acumen behind them— a lot of people cared. A hell of a lot of people.

Jake gave up pretending to be all casual and dispassionate. He flattened his sneakers to the parquet floor and shoved his chair backwards, leaping to his feet in a sharp movement. The chair continued its journey until it thumped gently against the wall, but by then Jake had already completed half a lap of the room's wall of windows.

'In a saturated marketplace, Jake, just having a great product isn't enough.' This came from the Vice President, Marketing & Communications, an elegant, spindly woman with jet-black hair. 'Unfortunately, early indications from our market research are that the Armada phone is generating little interest from consumers. Our US and Japanese competitors have the market cornered—people want the familiar brand, regardless of our superior phone.'

Jake paused. 'And what, exactly, do you think I could do about that? How is my mug on a magazine cover going to sell phones?'

The VP smiled. 'The results of our copy-testing focus groups are compelling. An advertisement including your name and photo scored significantly higher in brand linkage and consumer motivation. We're talking quadrupling of interest in the product.'

Jake didn't even bother being surprised that focus groups had been run. Of course they had. He was the only one late to this party.

He rubbed his forehead, a futile effort to erase the newly created furrows. His jaw was clamped shut and his teeth ground together.

'The board's recommendation is that we proceed with the Jake Donner campaign.' It was Cynthia again.

'If you decline, we'll be forced to reconvene to begin implementation of the company restructure,' added the CFO. *Restructure,* of course, being code for mass redundancies.

Now the VP chimed in. 'We're planning a short campaign, Jake. One month of inconvenience to you for tens of millions in potential increased revenue.'

The whole board murmured in enthusiastic agreement. Yes, this was definitely an ambush. He half expected them all to start lobbing their pens at him next—in a perfectly coordinated fashion, of course.

One month of inconvenience.

Could he do it? One month of shoehorning himself into whatever shiny package Marketing chose to squish him into? One month of posing and saying all the right things in aid of dragging Armada out of this financial hole?

One month for thousands of saved jobs and millions of dollars?

It didn't sound like much of a sacrifice when put like that. He might be far from the sole owner any more, but deep down inside he still considered Armada his. His responsibility. His employees.

Really, the decision was a no brainer.

Reluctantly, Jake grunted something that Cynthia correctly interpreted as acquiescence.

Well, he wasn't about to jump up and down in excitement, was he?

Something totally random occurred to him: *Lord. He'd better not have to wear a suit.*

Ella Cartwright waited patiently outside the boardroom's double doors, seated neatly on a low leather couch. Her black patent heels did *not* click nervously on the floorboards. Her fingers did not twist and tie themselves in knots on her lap. And she certainly didn't ask the CEO's personal assistant, who'd escorted her all the way to the twenty-sixth floor, any of the myriad questions about Jake Donner that sat on the tip of her tongue.

Not doing all those things was possible, of course, because *those* things she could control.

The butterflies currently tap-dancing in her tummy? Well, not so much.

But that was okay.

No one needed to know about them.

Finally, the doors were pushed open, and a parade of exquisitely suited executives slowly made their way out. Ella was on her feet well before she caught a flash of Cynthia George's distinctive red blazer amongst the mass of wintry black, grey and navy.

Ella allowed herself a fleeting moment of pride as she recognised the jacket she'd personally selected for Cynthia's revamped wardrobe. With her sharp haircut, flawlessly applied make-up and flattering outfit, Cynthia was a walking advertisement for Picture Perfect, Ella's five-year-old image consultancy firm.

But, while Cynthia's 'look' had needed a review, her communication—and negotiation—skills definitely hadn't. This had been demonstrated most effectively to Ella when she'd attempted to say no when she'd received Cynthia's most unexpected request.

Take on *Jake Donner* as a client?

Not in a million years.

Except—how to say no to your number one client with no reasonable excuse? Or rather, without a reason she had any intention of disclosing?

It turned out it wasn't possible. Even worse, Cynthia had made it clear that she considered this job a personal favour. And when half your clientele was a direct result of Cynthia's word of mouth, a favour was definitely not too much to ask.

And besides, if she was objective—even though the concept of objectivity was laughable where Jake was concerned—with Jake Donner she'd have a success story that would far eclipse Cynthia's. Her business was doing well, but with Jake on her client list the impact on her bottom line could be stratospheric.

The fact that Jake was the star of her number one most humiliating experience—and from a girl with quite a list, that was saying something—was completely irrelevant.

So here she was. Not—outwardly—nervous at all, just moments away from seeing Jake Donner for the first time in thirteen years.

To say she felt ill would be a monumental understatement.

'Ella!' Cynthia called, meeting Ella's gaze with typical direct-ness. 'Come in. I've asked Jake to stay back a few minutes.'

Behind Ella, a *ding* announced the arrival of the elevator, and within seconds the two women were alone in the hallway as the rest of the board were whisked away.

'How did the meeting go?' Ella asked.

But Cynthia only responded with matching raised eyebrows.

Seriously, what did Ella expect? Jake was Sydney's most famous recluse. He was about to be splashed across Australian and international media. He was not going to be in a good mood.

And when he saw her, it was only going to get worse. She had no doubt Jake wanted his past to stay as buried as hers.

With a deep breath, Ella straightened her shoulders, and men-tally yanked herself into line as Cynthia reopened the heavy boardroom doors.

She could do this. She was Ella Cartwright.

Confident. Polished. Successful.

Jake Donner was just another client.

Another deep breath.

You're not that girl any more.

Confident. Polished. Successful.

He probably barely remembered her.

Just another client.

Ella repeated the phrase over and over as she entered the room, scarcely acknowledging the expansive table that domi-nated the room or the drizzling rain that blurred the city vista. She was too busy focusing on the rear view of a dark head of slightly-too-long hair—all that was visible of Jake with his chair swivelled away from the doorway.

He didn't move as they approached.

'Well played, Cynthia,' he said, his tone quiet but not soft.

Ella blinked, taking a moment to absorb a voice both famil-iar and yet completely foreign. He'd been seventeen last time she'd seen him, his voice already deep and mature. But now it was…different. In a way that she couldn't quite explain. Richer, somehow.

For no reason she could fathom, she shivered.

'Not played, Jacob,' Cynthia said. 'That would imply I was the winner and you the loser. Unless, of course, you've cast Armada in the winner's role?'

Jake laughed, but still didn't turn. 'There's no guarantee this is going to work, Cynthia. I think everyone is hugely overestimating my appeal to the average Australian.'

Ella swallowed a surprised laugh. Surely Jake couldn't truly believe that? Despite her best efforts—her *very* best—avoiding Jake Donner entirely when she'd moved to Sydney almost a decade earlier had proved impossible. This might have been the first time they'd been in the same room, but Jake had permeated her world at all sorts of inopportune moments.

He was hard to miss, what with his success being the freakish type that attracted the mainstream media—with his name splashed across everything from articles of terribly serious business analysis to the trashiest of gossip magazines. And he was always linked to impressive phrases: *Internet Visionary* for one. Or *Web Evangelist*. Even *The Bill Gates of His Generation*.

She remembered thinking Jake would've got a kick out of that last one.

Belatedly, Ella registered that Cynthia was speaking. Introducing her.

As the chair began to turn Ella swallowed, then shut her eyes briefly, so by the time Jake Donner's ice-blue eyes locked with hers, she was ready.

Sort of.

'Good morning,' she said. 'I'm Ella Cartwright, owner of Picture Perfect. I'll be your personal rebranding and image consultant for the duration of the campaign.'

Good. She sounded every bit as professional—and *together*—as normal.

She could do this.

Ella stepped towards Jake, her hand extended, just as she would if he were any other brand-new client.

Which he was.

A moment passed. Nothing happened.

Had she made a tactical error, pretending she didn't know him? It was a risk. One she'd decided worth taking after her weekend of preparing for—read: stressing about—this meeting.

Her plan was simple: brazen it out, and hope for the best.

The alternative could not possibly be considered.

Jake's gaze was unreadable as the silence stretched. Stubbornly, Ella kept her hand right where it was, and her stare did not waver.

Not that it didn't want to. Her eyes wanted to drop to the floor—desperately. Her shoulders wanted to slouch. Her arms wanted to cross and form a useless shield.

And most of all, her body wanted to sprint as fast as her spiky heels would carry her—out of this room and infinitely far, far away.

But she'd never do any of those things. Not any more. The girl Jake had known would have. Definitely.

With no other option but to look at him, she did, her gaze travelling across a face—despite all the photos she'd seen of him over the years—that was still a surprise. He was just so different from the boy she remembered.

He was *more*. More broad, with muscles clearly outlined by the thin fabric of his T-shirt. More handsome, with any hint of softness long ago erased by the harsh angles of age, and a sharper edge to the line of his jaw to complement the hollowing out of his cheeks. And more dark, with his hair bereft of its splashes of sun-streaked blond and now simply the colour of her morning espresso.

She'd once thought him cute. Gorgeous, even. But that no longer covered it.

Devastatingly handsome came closer.

Finally, she let her hand drop. She smoothed it over her hip, the fine fabric of her wool pencil skirt just the slightest bit rough under her palm.

She nodded, a brisk, workmanlike movement. 'Well, then. I guess our first task will be to discuss the value of a good first impression.'

Again, she sounded absolutely normal. She even managed a smile, although her lips felt as if they stretched across her teeth.

Ella was definitely able to read Jake's expression clearly now: guarded and wary—following just the briefest flash of confusion.

'Is that your expert opinion.... *Ella?*'

She held her breath, sure Jake was going to announce that he already knew her. Reveal in one fell swoop the past she'd gone to such great lengths to hide—and to her star client, no less.

And then inspiration hit. She needed to talk to Jake—alone.

'It is,' she said. 'But don't worry,' she said, turning to Cynthia. 'I'll get him from surly to suave in no time.'

In her peripheral vision Ella was sure she saw Jake's jaw drop. He went to speak, but she cut him off.

'Actually, Cynthia—would you mind leaving us for a few minutes? I know this was supposed to be a brief meet and greet, but, really, there's no time like the present. And obviously we have *lots* of work to do.'

The older lady grinned. 'That you do,' she said, and her eyes were sparkling as she looked from Jake to Ella and back again. 'Good luck,' she whispered as she paused briefly beside Ella on her way out. 'Don't worry, he's not normally this prickly. He just needs a little time to adjust to his new role.'

If only that were the real reason Jake was currently near burning her skin with the intensity of his glare.

But Ella just laughed, smiling as if she were a woman with infallible confidence—and not at all concerned that she was about to be alone in a room with Jake Donner.

An instant later, as the door clicked shut, she was.

The next second he was on his feet. Then, suddenly—horribly—he was standing far too close to her. Close enough that she could smell the clean, fresh scent of him—not cologne, something else. Maybe whatever he washed his clothes in? An innocuous, friendly scent that did not match the reaction he triggered in her.

Blood thrummed through her veins and the hairs on her arms stood on end.

And then warmth collected low in her belly, the sensation shocking her. Surely he couldn't still affect her in that way? Hadn't she learnt the hard way what a mistake it was to want Jake Donner?

He waited before he spoke, for what felt like hours. Could he sense her tension, even though she did nothing—not a blink—to give herself away?

Finally, *finally,* he spoke.

'What the hell is going on, *Eleanor*?'

CHAPTER TWO

ELEANOR CARTWRIGHT.

Jake couldn't quite grasp the frankly crazy concept that the woman before him, this woman who didn't so much as flinch as he delivered his trademark—or so the papers said—glower, was Eleanor.

It didn't make any sense.

He'd recognised her immediately, of course.

Or maybe not immediately. All he'd heard was Cynthia starting to talk some rubbish about hiring him an image consultant— *an image consultant? That was a job?*—and then he'd turned around ready to tell this consultant that he had no requirement for her services. He'd barely been paying attention when Cynthia had mentioned the consultant's name, too focused on ending this latest bout of high-handedness as quickly as possible.

The board might have got away with it this morning—due to very specific extenuating circumstances—but Jake Donner did not get pushed around. He never had been, and he never would. It was yet another reason why he avoided the corporate world.

He had no time to pander to the whims of others.

But then, with the words *Unfortunately you've wasted your time* right on the tip of his tongue—he'd seen her.

His gaze had caught with hers, instantly. And his first reaction, if he were brutally honest, had been something hot, and primal, and male. His body had registered the obvious: a beautiful woman stood before him. A woman with brilliant emerald eyes and thick lashes of blackest black.

But then his mind had kicked into gear, and he'd recognised her.

It had been a long time. A very, very long time. Long enough that he couldn't remember the last time he'd thought of her.

But he hadn't forgotten Eleanor.

Although his memories clashed dramatically with the woman who stood before him now.

Because the transformation was complete.

Hair, teeth, glasses—lack of—*everything* had changed. Where Eleanor had once had nicely rounded curves she was now willowy, bordering on thin. Her dirty blonde hair had become auburn-streaked mahogany and her pale skin now had a golden hue. The braces were gone, the glasses as well, and—he was sure—she was wearing those coloured contact lenses. As at sixteen, Eleanor Cartwright's eyes had *definitely* been brown.

And finally, her nose... It was long, thin and *straight.* The bump she'd hated so much conspicuously absent.

At a glance, he'd been right—she *was* beautiful. But if you looked past the dazzling camouflage of her hair and make-up, the reality was quite different.

Full lips, but her mouth veered closer to wide than delicate. And while she did have defined cheekbones, her jaw was strong, not elegant. Plus her eyes, once you saw beyond all the make-up, were pretty, but certainly not spectacular.

So, no, she wasn't beautiful, if you really looked. But as a whole package—from her perfectly fitted suit, to the soft elegance of her upswept hair and the aura of confidence she just oozed from every pore—it would be easy to think she was.

She still hadn't answered his question.

'Eleanor—'

'That's not my name,' she said. Snapped, really.

She gave a little shake of her head and stepped around him, covering the short distance to the table in three hip-swinging strides. She turned, leaning her butt against the table, her hands lightly resting on either side of her on the polished wood surface, her ankles casually crossed.

'I thought the answer was obvious,' she said. 'I'm an image

consultant. You need your image to be made over—*quickly*—so, tada! Here I am. Image consultant at your service.'

He was a little in awe at her unflappable demeanour. Oh, he knew she wasn't as calm as she appeared. He'd seen the flicker in her eyes when he'd stepped too close.

But she was determined to give nothing else away.

'What's with ignoring the elephant in the room, Eleanor?' he said. 'Don't play games. We're not strangers.'

No, definitely not strangers.

But certainly not friends. The room hummed with uncomfortable tension.

She shrugged. 'I fail to see how our past is relevant. I'm a professional. You're a professional. I can see no reason why anything but the here and now would be of any importance.'

However, what *was* relevant was his sudden urge to end this meeting—and this whole *image consultant* debacle. Immediately.

'Eleanor—'

She groaned and shook her head. 'Really? You think the fact I had a crush on you—when I was a very silly and very angst-ridden teenage girl, no less—would matter now? I assure you, I'm not secretly carrying a thirteen-year-old torch.' A pause. 'Don't worry, you're safe. You're in no imminent danger of further declarations of love.'

That hadn't been what he'd been thinking at all. He'd been thinking that there was a woman in his boardroom who made him feel...

Lord, he didn't know. Made him feel as if he didn't want to be in the same room with her any more.

The issue didn't need any further analysis than that.

The benefit of being very wealthy—and known for being, well, surly, as Eleanor had said—was that he didn't need to do any of this. He didn't even need to worry about a carefully polite excuse. He could tell her to leave, give no explanation, and that would be that.

A very silly and very angst-ridden teenage girl.

Jake had no idea why her words were echoing in his brain.

She was wrong, too. He remembered strength. And pain. And…
Need.

She'd needed him.

Just like…

The words he'd had piled up and waiting on the tip of his tongue—to end this unwanted, awkward meeting—stalled.

Jake watched her watching him. Had she guessed what he was about to say? He thought so.

And she wouldn't just meekly leave; he knew it, absolutely. She was different—and it wasn't just her clothes, or her hair. This Eleanor studied him with a hard edge he never would've imagined her capable of.

He couldn't even begin to reconcile his memories with the woman standing before him now.

It was as if she were a different person. Certainly not Eleanor, his best friend through those awkward high-school years when they'd both been painfully stereotypical social pariahs.

They'd been straight out of Central Casting. Jake was The Geek, while Eleanor had been The Wallflower.

With no other friends, they'd initially banded together through necessity, the only two students on scholarships at their fancy private school—low socio-economic ones, too, just for that added stigma. The only two students who lived in government-subsidised housing, and the only two students with eccentric new-age parents—hers—or a drug-addled verging-on-neglectful mother—his.

Eleanor's words still hung in the air between them.

'So what you're saying is that you're not interested in a walk down memory lane. As far as you're concerned, we met five minutes ago.'

That wasn't even close to what he'd meant to say. *Those* words, waiting too long, had evaporated.

She beamed—but was her smile brittle? 'Exactly.'

'That's kind of nuts.'

This was kind of nuts.

She blinked, but smiled on, undeterred. 'That's your opinion. Personally, that's what I'd call dwelling on our past as—clearly—

we've both moved on. I don't remember either of us sending Christmas cards.'

Touché.

Yet, he still didn't know quite what to make of this situation. He wanted her to leave—but didn't.

His confusion bothered him—after all, Jake Donner thought in black and white. Binary ones and zeros.

He'd never thought he'd see her again. It was a shock...no. Not even that. A surprise. Combined with the recently completed board meeting, it was hardly unexpected that his thought process would be a little...muddled.

But, one thing was clear.

'Here,' he said, 'I'm going to make this easy. I don't want an image consultant. So I'll tell Cynthia, and—'

'No!'

It was by far and away the most expressive word she'd uttered so far.

He watched her as she took a deep breath and rolled her shoulders slightly. 'I mean, that's unnecessary. I'm an experienced image consultant, Jake, with one hundred per cent positive feedback from my clients,' she said. 'My firm isn't the biggest, but my track record is outstanding. As you know, Cynthia is one of my clients. But I've also assisted some of the most famous and powerful people in Sydney.'

She listed a few names, from singers, to television journalists to chief executives.

'I assure you, you won't find anyone better qualified than myself to help you,' she said, finishing her little pitch.

'That's all well and good,' he said, 'but what if I don't think I need an image consultant at all?'

She laughed, the first time her expression had diversified from its mask of professionalism.

Jake crossed his arms defensively, but he refused to ask for the cause of her mirth. He had no doubt she was about to tell him.

Just as soon as she—finally—stopped laughing.

* * *

Ella did her very best to silence the last little hiccups of laughter, frankly appalled at her reaction.

What had happened to Jake being 'just another client'? As if she'd ever fall into fits of giggles with anyone else.

It was basically Image Consultant 101: Don't laugh at your client. Ever.

Not exactly the ideal way to build up someone's self-confidence, was it? And that was kind of the whole point of her job.

More importantly—he already didn't want anything to do with her. It radiated from him in waves.

So, yeah, hysterical giggles were far from the most intelligent way to change his mind.

She cleared her throat. 'Sorry,' she said. 'That was uncalled for.'

Jake was obviously waiting for her to elaborate, watching her with an oddly contradictory intensity—as if he was pushing her away while simultaneously filing her somewhere for future reference. Whatever it was, it did all sorts of unwanted things to her equilibrium.

Which just wasn't acceptable. She'd learnt years ago how to present herself at her absolute best in *all* situations. The old Eleanor would've ducked her chin, and slouched, and blushed under the intensity of Jake's attention.

It bothered the new Ella that her body was trying its best to do *all* those things. She couldn't remember the last time she'd had to fight to project the confident, polished image she'd so carefully crafted.

It had been long enough that she hadn't thought she was pretending any more—that she just *was* Ella. But five minutes with Jake and if she wasn't careful, she'd be sixteen again.

And she was *never* going to let that happen.

Deliberately, she restraightened her already perfectly straight shoulders. Took a deep breath. Remembered the affirmations she'd once stuck to her bathroom mirror:

Confident. Polished. Successful.

'Jake, you're a walking "Before Picture". Look at you,' she

said—and she was relieved her voice was back to cool and collected. 'Hair that you don't cut often enough—and I'd guess that when you do you go to those "no need to book" salons?' Jake's stony lack of denial she interpreted as a *yes*. 'You're wearing a T-shirt that looks at least five years old, your jeans have a rip in them, and to say your shoes were scuffed would be kind.'

To be fair, he did look rather hot in his super, super casual get-up—the well-washed pale grey fabric of his shirt outlining the strength of his chest, and the worn jeans hanging low on his hips. But an image that was going to sell millions of phones for Armada? No, not so much. Unless Armada's new corporate look was 'scruffy'.

Jake crossed his arms in a slow, deliberate movement. 'So I'll go shopping.'

Ella took a measured breath.

'To someone unfamiliar with the importance of personal appearance in the corporate world, I can see how my services may seem easily replaced by a trip to your local shopping centre.' She paused, skimming her gaze down Jake's lean form. 'However, over the next few weeks I'll demonstrate to you the transformational impact of personal image. We'll also explore and develop your own personal brand through my media-training services.'

Jake's expression was someplace between scepticism and contempt. 'Personal *brand*, Eleanor—really? People actually talk like that, and think it means—or makes a difference to— anything?'

'Yes,' she said, refusing to be rattled. 'People do. Many people. And while you may be in denial you do need my help. Help with your image—and the way you handle the media and the general public. Open and approachable are not two words anyone would ever associate with you.'

'I wouldn't want them to,' he said. 'My life is my business.'

'Of course it is,' Ella said. 'And with my assistance, you'll have far more control over the pieces of your life you choose to reveal—and those you choose to keep private.'

To hide.

Jake shrugged dismissively. 'You're a bit too late for that.

The media dug up my past years ago. They can write what they like. I'm just not going to help them out.'

He was right. The media had splashed his past across the more tabloid of Australia's newspapers and magazines. The disadvantaged childhood. The prescription drug-addicted mother. The absent father who'd squeezed every cent he could out of Jake's fame by talking to any magazine that approached him.

And, of course, the women he'd dated. More than one had sold their stories within what must have been moments of the end of their liaison with Jake.

Although, come to think of it, Ella couldn't remember the last time she'd seen that type of article. Did he have a girlfriend now?

No. He was just another client.

It wasn't any of her business.

'If you give them something, Jake, you can take back control. The media won't need to write lies in place of a truth you give them.'

He shook his head, rejecting her words.

'There's no avoiding it, Jake—the media is key to this campaign. So you're going to have to learn to play the game for a few weeks.'

'I'm not a child,' Jake said, walking past her and closer to the windows. The rain had become heavier and so Jake was gazing at little more than a wall of water. 'I can play nice. I don't need lessons.'

This time the smallest of frustrated sighs did slip out. 'You're committed to the campaign. And my services *will* make a difference. I promise you that, after a few sessions with me, you'll barely recognise yourself.'

He met her gaze. 'That's exactly what I'm worried about.'

She blinked. Normally her clients couldn't wait to begin their transformation. Ella understood that, understood the need to grow and change. Jake—so apparently happy to ignore what the rest of the world thought of him, and so reluctant to concede anything to conform—she had a lot of trouble getting her head around.

She always had. In that way, at least, he hadn't changed at all.

But she could do this. She had to.

'While it would appear I'm not going to convince you today—I will convince you. You need me, Jake.'

With his back to her, Jake shrugged. 'I seriously doubt that.'

Ella's jaw clenched.

'Give me two hours.'

He turned back towards her, a rapid movement in stark contrast to his default speed of languid. Maybe, finally, she'd piqued his interest. 'For what?'

'Proof,' she said. She mimicked his casual shrug of before. 'That's all.'

'And if you fail—that's it. You'll walk away—leaving me image-consultant free?'

She nodded. 'Exactly. Although it's possible the Armada board may disagree with this arrangement.'

Disagree was probably too soft a word. 'Have conniptions' would more likely be their response at the prospect of Jake Donner—with no buffing or polishing—fronting their campaign.

But, of course, it wouldn't get to that.

Jake made a flippant gesture. 'I'll handle the board.'

Ella's lips tipped up into the tightest of grins. 'So, we have a deal? Two hours of your time. If I'm right, you agree to follow my programme. If I'm wrong—that's it. Armada can tear up my contract.'

Slowly, he nodded. Then closed the distance between them and held out his hand.

Ah. Now he was going to shake her hand—when he thought she'd just made a deal she was certain to lose.

Had he seriously forgotten how competitive she was? Losing was never an option for Ella Cartwright.

But Jake's touch suddenly obliterated any thoughts of victory or defeat.

It was a simple movement: just a handshake. Yet the sensation of his palm, and his fingers—large and just the slightest bit rough—wrapped around hers, it…struck her momentarily dumb. All she could concentrate on was the warmth radiating from this very G-rated connection. The sparks…

'Why are you so determined to work with me?'

Ella snatched her hand away. No. Regressing back to a gooey, lovesick teenager was so not an option.

'Because any image consultant worth her salt would want to work with you. High-profile client, high-profile campaign— what more could I ask for?' Then she added, because she didn't think she could reiterate it enough, 'The fact we were once friends has absolutely no relevance. This is a business relationship, pure and simple.'

It was just slightly catastrophic that Cynthia had insisted it exist at all.

Jake met her gaze and just looked at her for a long moment. He didn't waver from her eyes, but Ella still had the sense he was searching. Exploring.

'Are you sure that's it?' he asked.

'Of course,' she replied. Firmly, without missing a beat.

Because she was sure. Absolutely sure.

It was time for her to go.

'I'll contact your PA to organise our two hours for tomorrow.'

'Tomorrow?'

'We could do today, if you prefer,' she said. Sweetly.

Ella was nearly positive she saw Jake grin—just a little.

As long as she remembered to treat him exactly as who he was: a client, and she continued to diligently leave the past exactly where it belonged, this could actually work out okay.

It could. Kind of like how pigs could—theoretically—fly right past this twenty-sixth floor window.

'No,' he said. 'Tomorrow is fine.'

'Excellent,' Ella said—briskly and with utter professionalism.

She excused herself and exited the Armada building just as briskly and professionally.

And to look at her, absolutely no one would ever know, or even suspect, how much she was shaking inside.

What had she just got herself into?

CHAPTER THREE

THE next day, Ella stepped out of one of the Armada building's high-rise elevators onto the charcoal-flecked white marble tiles that paved the lobby of Jake's floor. *Armada* shouted out to her in foot-high mirrored letters above the reception desk, and every piece of furniture in the vicinity seemed to be made out of glass or chrome. It was all very…shiny.

Somehow she'd expected something different of this space—something different from the rest of the corporation's building. Jake's PA had explained that it was the developers' floor—basically the place where all the geeks like Jake worked. Although, of course, his PA hadn't called them geeks. She'd used words like *software engineers* and *system architects,* all of which had whizzed right over Ella's head.

But effectively, this was Jake's domain—and it just wasn't what she'd expected. With all its hard edges and heavy aura of obscene wealth, it didn't seem to fit with the guy who'd worn faded jeans to an executive board meeting.

This whole building just wasn't where she'd imagined Jake would end up—the boy who'd first earned her awe with his skill with those ancient computer games they'd played on his mother's unreliable, flickering TV. Even back then, in the early nineties, he'd dismantled and tinkered—always needing to know how things worked. He'd built things, too. As soon as their school had internet, he'd been there at the library, figuring out how to build a web page. And then software that actually *did stuff.* Although she'd never really understood how it all worked—she'd been so easily impressed—a little counter on his web page that counted down the days to her birthday had wowed her far more than the pages and pages of programming code he was so proud of.

She gave her name to one of the handful of efficient-looking receptionists, and then took a seat on an uncomfortable white leather couch—with shiny chrome feet and armrests, of course. Beside her, floor-to-ceiling windows gave her a clear view down to the Royal Botanic Gardens, although she could see only glimpses of the harbour, what with the surrounding skyscrapers acting like splayed fingers across her eyes.

The sound of footsteps drew her gaze back into the room, and there was Jake.

In a variation of what he'd worn yesterday, but this time his jeans were dark grey, and his white T-shirt had a complicated logo splashed across the front of it.

Without thinking, she smiled—not a businesslike, work-appropriate smile, but a big, cheesy grin. Even if his outfit broke every one of her executive style guidelines, *this* was the Jake she remembered. It was an unexpectedly reassuring contrast in this environment of austerity and high gloss.

For an instant—so quickly gone that she was almost sure she'd imagined it—he smiled back. And then his gaze drifted to the camera bag at her feet, and his lips thinned.

'Let me guess—you're not carrying that camera around for the fun of it?'

No hello, no nothing.

Bringing her grin down a lot of notches—to determinedly cheery rather than genuinely cheesy—she replied, 'Nope. You and this camera will be seeing a lot of each other over the next couple of hours.'

His lips managed to get even thinner. 'Fine. Let's get this over with.'

The cool words were just the reminder she needed. Jake was no more the boy who'd once lived in the fibro house with the overgrown lawn than she was the girl in the multicoloured weatherboard cottage next door. And right now, he was *not* pleased.

She toned down her smile even further—to bland—and smoothed her palms down the back of her skirt as she stood. She grabbed her handbag and hooked the heavy camera bag over her shoulder.

Jake muttered something under his breath that sounded something like *total waste of time.*

She simultaneously bristled and ignored him.

His conviction that he didn't need her was, almost, a little endearing. He really had absolutely no idea. But he would—very soon.

So she didn't bite.

'Brilliant,' she said. 'Lead the way.'

Without a word he led her down a corridor lined with meeting rooms, all but one empty. Through the nearly opaque glass she could see an enthusiastic meeting in progress, and, from what she could surmise given her blurry view, all attendees were dressed just as casually as Jake.

'So the dress code on this floor is "jeans"?' she asked Jake's back as he strode ahead.

'My staff can wear whatever they like,' Jake replied. 'What they achieve is more important to me than what they look like.'

'Dressing professionally is about more than just looking good,' she pointed out.

Jake didn't even bother to look over his shoulder. 'They're just clothes,' he said, in a frustratingly dismissive tone.

But again she held her tongue. After today she'd have many opportunities to change his opinion.

At the end of the hallway, Jake opened a heavy door, holding it open to let her walk in ahead of him.

It wasn't a small door—quite the opposite in fact—and yet Ella found herself hesitating.

Why?

He wasn't crowding her, he wasn't doing a thing but stand there. But he was tall, and broad—just *big*—and even in jeans his presence felt far from relaxed. Literally and figuratively, he filled the space around him.

You're being ridiculous.

But it was as if suddenly every cell in her body were aware of him and, as a result, she'd apparently lost her ability to move.

If she waited another nanosecond, he was going to notice. And that would hardly help the situation if he knew exactly how effortlessly he pushed her off balance.

So she took a deep breath. And walked past him.

There. That wasn't so hard, was it?

She mentally smacked herself in the forehead as he closed the door and his deep voice directed her to take a seat.

She *really* needed to pull herself together. She was as jittery as…well, whatever was jittery enough to overthink walking through a doorway.

She sank into a red leather chair across from a glass and stainless-steel desk. The whole office looked like an explosion of dot-com clichés—multicoloured couches grouped in a corner, a mini basketball ring above the bin, a football table in front of the panoramic windows. There was even one of those magic eight balls on the desktop.

'Great office,' she said, because it was. Although, once again, she had an odd sense of incongruence, as if Jake didn't quite belong.

He shrugged, arranging himself in his chair across from her: one shoulder propped against its back, his backside dangerously close to the edge of the seat, one leg thrown out stretched, the other bent haphazardly at the knee. *Sprawled* would be an apt description.

All dark and broody, he did *sprawled* well.

'Armada hired some fancy interior designer,' he said with derision, dismissing the room with barely a glance

Ah. That made sense. And again she was oddly reassured that this *wasn't* Jake—a crazy reaction, given her role was to help Jake fit better into exactly this type of environment.

Ella tugged at the houndstooth fabric of the hem of her skirt, her knees pressed together primly, her back ramrod straight.

She was acting as if she were at a job interview, she realised.

All nervous and fidgety. All *Eleanor.*

And that just wasn't on.

Once again, she repeated that reminder
together.

This was not a big deal. He was just another client.

A brilliant addition to her growing list of success stories. As
she'd reminded herself repeatedly in her middlingly convincing
pep talk on the train that morning.

If she focused on that—and not their past—she'd have no
problems at all. And with that in mind, she deliberately smiled
her most welcoming smile.

Jake raised an eyebrow, but she chose to ignore that.

'So, what we're going to do this morning is have a mock interview. I'm going to ask you a few questions, and film your
responses. Then we'll watch the footage back together, and I'll
identify areas where I can assist you.'

Jake looked less than enthusiastic, but at least he didn't argue.

He continued to convey general lack of interest as she set
up the tripod, although he did perk up a little when the camera came out.

'What kind of camera's that?' he asked as she bent and fid-
dled with the equipment.

Ah. Always such a techno geek. Trust Jake to be interested
in this shiny, state-of-the-art example of technological wizardry.

'It's a digital SLR that also shoots video,' Ella said. 'Normally
when I do these shoots with clients I have a proper set-up with
a journalist, lights and a cameraman. Helps to create the sense
of a real interview. But for today, this will do.'

He frowned. 'There wasn't time to organise all that?'

'I thought you'd prefer something a little more low-key,' she
said, although until right this second she hadn't truly considered
why she'd thought that.

'Thank you,' he said gruffly, surprising her.

She finished securing the camera and met his eyes across the
wide glass table. 'No worries.'

He didn't manage to crack a smile—but something had definitely softened in his gaze. Well, at the very least, now he looked
marginally less likely to grunt his way through the upcoming
mock interview.

Soon everything was in place, Jake remaining behind his desk with Ella and the camera across from him. She'd considered relocating to the comfy-looking couches across the room, but figured that a desk between them was probably the better idea. She didn't need a repeat of that awkward moment at the door. Or even her reaction to his touch when he'd shook her hand yesterday. Maximum distance between her and Jake could only be a good thing for her sanity.

'Let's start with a few warm-up questions, just to get you started. Pretend I'm interviewing you in a television studio.' Ella put on her best interviewer voice. 'So tell me, Jake, what did you have for breakfast?'

He blinked. 'Is this really necessary?'

Ella nodded. 'Trust me. It'll help you get used to the camera.'

'Toast,' he said.

'Interesting. And what did you have on your toast today, Jake?'

'This is riveting,' Jake said, with absolutely zero expression. 'Surely we can do better than this?'

In reply she just watched him steadily, and finally he sighed, and then spoke. 'Vegemite and cheese.'

Obviously, some things never changed.

'Tell me a little more—'

'What are you grinning about?'

Ella hadn't even realised she was smiling. 'Pardon me?'

'Come on, share the joke.'

He didn't sound defensive—a welcome change. Just curious.

'Oh. I guess I was remembering you and your breakfast feasts. I thought you had hollow legs, the amount of bread you went through.'

Ella carefully rearranged her face back to *serious interviewer*. They needed to focus—plus she was not in the habit of talking about old memories. Ever. 'As I was saying, tell me a little—'

'Do you still have the same breakfast? It was Froot Loops, right?'

He'd remembered. Before she could stop herself, she smiled again—but bit her lip as soon as she realised.

How dumb to be pleased he remembered something as stupid as her favourite cereal.

'Of course not,' she said briskly. 'It's pure sugar. I'm careful to follow a low-fat, low-sugar, whole-food diet.'

'That sounds terribly boring.'

To be honest, it kind of was. But it was the only possible way she could stay a size ten. And she wasn't about to give that up.

She shrugged. 'You'd be surprised how varied and satisfying it is—and it's so good for my health and well-being.'

Now she sounded like a rather dodgy advertisement for a miracle weight loss solution.

'Look, let's get back to the questions. Tell me—'

'New breakfast. New name. What's with the *Ella* thing, anyway?'

She sighed. 'Jake, I'm not the one being interviewed here.' She tilted her head in the direction of the camera beside her. 'Remember? This is about *you.*'

He shrugged unapologetically. 'Consider this part of the warm up? Besides, I would've thought you'd like me to build a rapport with my interviewers.'

She couldn't really argue with that. Then he put his palm to his chest. 'Hand on my heart, I promise I won't interrupt you again.' And then he smiled a knee-melting smile that made her seriously glad she was sitting down.

Words tumbled from her mouth. 'I never liked the name Eleanor. I changed it by deed poll years ago.'

She blinked. *Damn.* She shouldn't be talking to Jake like this. After all, he'd lost the right to ask her personal questions a long time ago.

More importantly, she reminded herself, he was her client.

Armada wasn't paying her to sit around and chat.

On the plus side—if he smiled like *that* at a female interviewer, Ella reckoned he could make anyone forget whatever curly question they'd thrown at him.

Ella dismissed the way her body instantly tensed at that idea as pure frustration, and *not* ridiculously placed jealousy related to hypothetical future interviews.

He nodded. 'And you changed pretty much everything else, too, I've noticed.' His gaze travelled over her—her hair, her impeccably made-up face, her perfectly fitted outfit.

Though she knew it was terrible, she all but preened under his gaze.

See, I can scrub up okay. I'm not a clumsy schoolgirl with bad hair any more.

But—strangely—he didn't look all that impressed. If anything, his expression was...disappointed?

Which was crazy. No one could possibly argue that she hadn't improved every single aspect of herself since the last time she'd seen Jake. She'd changed everything—and for the better.

She shifted awkwardly in her seat, then stilled her fingers when she realised she was plucking absently at the fabric of her skirt.

'Jake, can you tell me what makes the new Armada phone so special?'

He raised an eyebrow at the swift change of subject, but, thankfully, didn't call her on it.

Instead, almost instantly, he became more animated. He launched into a detailed—far too detailed, really—description of the phone, and his pet topic the operating system, which, she knew from Cynthia's briefing, was his brainchild.

For the next few minutes, Ella absorbed all she ever—ever—needed to know about *multi-touch capability, near field communications, API support* and *the team's focus on usability.* His detailed description went on and on—and eventually, she yawned.

'Am I boring you?'

She nodded emphatically.

'Lots of people are interested in that stuff,' Jake said, back to being just the slightest bit defensive.

'Not the average consumer,' Ella said. When he opened his mouth—to argue, she was sure—she took much enjoyment in being the one to interrupt this time. 'Put it this way. Do you want to hear me wax lyrical about my whole-food diet?'

He blanched.

'Exactly. Your multi-field-API whatsit…' her deliberate mangling of the secret language of software developers made him flinch '…is like my discussion on the health benefits of spelt. Only a very specific type of person is interested. And that person is *not* the average Australian.'

He nodded—reluctantly.

'How about I ask you a question that people will *really* want to know about "Sydney's reclusive millionaire"—'

'I'd rather you didn't call me that.'

'I'd rather you didn't interrupt me. You promised, remember?'

He gave the slightest of grins, and again she needed to bite her lip.

It was unexpected—this…what? Friendly conversation? Banter?

No. No. They were building a *rapport,* just as he'd said. That was all.

She took a deep breath. 'You're renowned for refusing to do interviews. What's changed?'

Jake immediately swung back to the defensive—this time, *very* defensive. 'I'm here to talk about the Armada phone. Not about myself.'

Undeterred, Ella carried on, now sticking determinedly to her interviewer persona. 'But, Jake, all our viewers are equally interested in *you.*'

'You know the answer, Ella. I'm sure Cynthia told you.'

'Pretend I'm an interviewer, Jake. Not Eleanor.'

Jake stared at her for a long moment. *What?*

'Eleanor?'

Too late she realised her mistake. One she'd never, ever made before.

'*Ella,*' she said. 'Of course that's what I meant.'

As he watched her Ella felt her cheeks grow steadily warmer, until she was *very* glad she wasn't the one with the camera pointed in her direction.

She bit her lip, trying to refocus. Remember where she was. And, more importantly, *who* she was. She was Ella Cartwright— successful, confident, popular.

Ella Cartwright: businesswoman, friend, girlfriend, even—sometimes. For very short periods. Her career always came first. Always.

But what she was not—not even in the slightest—was Eleanor.

'Freudian slip?' Jake asked.

'Not at all. My subconscious is obviously a little confused. When I knew you, I was Eleanor.' She shrugged, attempting nonchalance despite the tomato-hue of her cheeks and the whirring of her brain.

'You act like Eleanor's an entirely different person.'

'She is,' she said. Firmly. 'Now. I'm doing the interviewing, not you.'

'I liked Eleanor,' Jake said, ignoring her.

'No, you didn't,' she said, quickly, before her distracted brain could halt her tongue.

But it was true. He'd made his dislike quite clear that night, in his bedroom. And then confirmed it when he left Perth, and her life, without a backward glance.

For weeks—months—she'd expected *something*. An email maybe, so she'd checked the computers at school religiously each day. Or a phone call—and for far too long she'd leapt to her feet whenever its ring had reverberated throughout her wooden-framed house.

Really, she would've been happy with a postcard of the harbour bridge, even.

She'd been totally pathetic.

And now she was horrified to register an echo of that ache she'd forcibly buried so long ago. It had faded, for sure, but it was still there. Somewhere inside her.

A little piece of who she once was. Of the girl that Jake had rejected.

That *everyone* had rejected.

The realisation shocked her.

'Ella,' he said, and his voice was far too kind. 'You can't possibly—'

No. She didn't want to hear this. It should be impossible to remember his pity-edged tone from thirteen years ago but she did, and she didn't want to hear it again. 'When will the phone be available for purchase?' she said, snatching up a question at random.

There was a long silence, and Jake's brow furrowed as he studied her.

Surely he wouldn't push? What was the point? If there'd been anything worth saying, or saving, between them, it would've been said and done long ago.

Eventually, finally, he answered. 'The Armada phone will be launched worldwide on the first of August...'

And just like that, they were back on track. She was Ella, and he was Jake—her client. Only. Because that was the way it had to stay.

The way it was *going* to stay.

Jake tried—he really did—to pay attention.

It shouldn't have been too difficult a task, as Ella was sitting a perfectly respectable distance away from him. Given the huge size of his LED computer screen—about the only thing he actually *liked* in his office—their chairs weren't exactly shoved close together behind his desk. And yet, without the barrier of the desk between them, her nearness was distracting.

Currently she was possibly talking about the mock interview. But he couldn't be absolutely sure.

He'd been right, yesterday. This was not a good idea.

He was still uneasy in a room alone with Ella Cartwright.

What he wasn't—was any closer to understanding *why*.

She'd been right, logically. There must be a reason their friendship had ended with such finality. That he'd never been tempted to seek her out.

Nothing.

And yet, here they were, with definite undercurrents beneath every word they said, despite Ella's absolute insistence that this was nothing more than a business relationship.

Why had he even agreed to this?

It was a total waste of time, only prolonging the inevitable. He didn't need an image consultant.

He didn't need Ella back in his life.

Although even yesterday, even as he'd been telling her he didn't require her services, he'd been considering the possibility of asking her out for a—*platonic*—drink. A catch up between old friends. That was all. An hour or two of his life to get this weird imbalance out of his system.

Maybe he should still do that, once this was over. A means to an end, so to speak.

Because despite his best efforts, in the less than twenty-four hours since she'd walked back into his life, he'd spent *way* too much time thinking about her. Wondering. How could she possibly have changed so much?

Although—now and again, little actions had triggered half-forgotten memories. The way she tucked her hair behind her ears. The way, when the questions had turned to her, her gaze had skittered all over the room.

But for every glimpse that was familiar, there was so much that was not. Like her emerald green eyes, the freckle-free skin and her sexy-as-hell fire-engine-red lips.

Momentarily, there was absolutely no confusion for the cause of tension in the room. For now, he was back to basics.

'Jake,' she said, 'have you heard anything I've said?'

His gaze darted up from her mouth to her eyes and he watched as her cheeks went pink.

Ah. He remembered that blush, too.

She must have seen something of his very much work-inappropriate thoughts in his eyes, and her blush only deepened. Those thoughts, he remembered too—although thirteen-odd years ago, she'd been wearing a school uniform when she'd triggered them, not a tailored suit and three-inch heels.

Oh, yeah. He *had* liked Eleanor. A lot.

And all grown up, she was having a similar effect.

Which wasn't ideal.

Ha! No, that was a pretty pedestrian description.

Ella was a distraction he couldn't afford.

He needed to focus on the campaign, and on Armada. Besides, they both knew far too much about each other—each at their most vulnerable and most awkward. Anything between them would be the very definition of complicated and he didn't do complicated.

He did fun and temporary and unashamedly shallow.

His one long-term relationship had ended right around the time Georgina had felt the need to stumble about in his past, desperate to know—to *understand*, she'd said—all of him. His deadbeat dad and pastiche of a mother inexplicably her topics of choice.

But seriously, who wanted to discuss a dad who, when he was aged five, walked out without a backward glance? Not exactly a conversation to set a romantic mood, right?

As for his mother. Oh, the allure of the antics of Mrs Diana Donner. His favourite being that time he'd walked across the stage to accept a Maths prize, age thirteen. And in she'd staggered through the doors of the school gymnasium in nightie and bathrobe, barefoot, and with some indescribable substance down her front, quite possibly vomit, screaming out her love for him for all to hear and see.

So no. Not stories he had any interest in sharing with the women he…*saw*…he guessed was the appropriate term. Certainly didn't have relationships with.

But the thing was, Ella already knew them all. All the stories.

That didn't sit well with him.

'You're right, I wasn't paying attention,' he said, wrestling himself back on track. 'I'm still unconvinced I need to know any of this.'

It was difficult not to smile, despite the crackling tension, when right on cue her eyes flashed with irritation. Eleanor—no, *Ella,* he had to remember that—had always been so, so easy to get a rise out of.

'If you were paying attention, you would be convinced by now.'

He shrugged, and her whole body went rigid. One of her legs bounced a few times as she tapped her heel impatiently against

the marble floor—before she realised what she was doing and
went still. Then she turned to him, and smiled the widest, most
perfect and most plastic of smiles.

It was far from the first time she'd bestowed this smile upon
him in the past two days, and yet it still had the power to make
him tense. It was so false—and just so different from the easy,
crooked, Eleanor smile he was shocked to realise he remembered so vividly.

'What we're going to do now is watch your mock interview
from beginning to end, and I'll pause and make comments as
we go through. Any questions, feel free to ask.'

She didn't bother to wait for his agreement, and instead
reached forward to click the mouse, and start the camera she'd
connected to his computer earlier.

Jake settled back into his seat, determined to concentrate.
He'd promised Ella these two hours, and so he had to at least
try, even if he already knew the outcome.

Jake Donner definitely didn't need an image consultant.

Ella fast-forwarded through the warm-up questions. He
almost said something, tempted to tease her about her discom-
fort when the questions had turned to her—but then his head and
shoulders filled almost the entire screen and the words stalled
in his throat.

'You actually weren't too bad,' Ella was saying, watching the
screen. 'But I'm still confident that I'll be able to help you—and
Armada—really shine on camera.'

When he remained silent, Ella turned slightly in her chair to
look at him. 'Jake?'

'I look awful,' he said, surprising himself. After all, he wasn't
supposed to care about all this image rubbish.

Ella smiled. 'You look like a slightly grumpy guy with over-
long hair who doesn't like being interviewed. Plus, you kind of
sound like a mega geek.'

'Exactly.'

'And you now think that's a problem?'

He rubbed his temples. He'd actually been trying, really trying—wanting to prove Ella wrong. So he'd stuck to the sound

bites that Marketing had briefed him with—mostly. And he'd been really careful to keep his eyes on the camera. He'd been going for relaxed, but informative.

Instead, he'd ended up with—well, Ella got it right. Grumpy nerd. Even he was bored hearing himself go on about his precious phone.

He reached across Ella to grab the mouse. He didn't need to see any more.

Even though he didn't touch her, Ella leapt away as if she was afraid he would, forcing her chair to roll back a metre or so. She immediately recovered, calmly sliding her chair forward and pretending she hadn't moved at all. 'Don't be so hard on yourself,' she said brightly. 'I think we can work on the laconic look.' She meant the way he'd slouched in his chair. 'And you've actually got a really great natural presence on camera. That's not something everyone has.'

This made him feel a little better. 'Really?' he asked, still close to her as he clicked the mouse to close the video. 'Presence, huh?' He met her gaze, ridiculously pleased.

She reached out, pushing his shoulder lightly. 'Don't be too smug. You're still a grumpy geek—just with presence.'

He could see the moment she registered that she was touching him. Her eyes, with those super thick painted lashes, widened— and she went perfectly still.

Her hand fell away. 'Anyway. What I'm trying to say is there's lots there we can work with.'

Every word she said was spoken just a little faster than the one before it. Normally she was almost defiantly professional— now she was having trouble even looking at him.

It wasn't very smart of him and it was definitely pointless but he was liking this effect he had on her. That the zing he'd felt when they'd touched was not even close to one way.

'Give me an example,' he said. 'One of your image slash personal rebranding consultant pieces of wisdom.'

'Wait,' she said. 'Does this mean I've convinced you?'

She'd regrouped, and now she looked him dead in the eye, the mask back in place. Her expression revealed nothing.

'Not yet. I need a...' He very nearly said *taste,* but his brain put the skids on just in time. Not that the idea didn't refuse to dislodge. '...sample.'

Although of course he wasn't thinking about samples as he looked at her. Not at all.

This was crazy.

He was hardly some sex-starved pariah. Sure, it had been a few months since he'd had a date, but that was entirely his own decision. And thoughts of tasting the lips of Eleanor Cartwright—of all people—were just wrong.

His PA had been hassling him to go on a blind date with a friend of hers. Maybe he should take her up on the offer.

'Well,' Ella said, and her tongue peeked out to lick her lips. Instantly she had his full attention. 'It's good that you kept your eyes on the camera. But you were a little intense. You need to give the viewer a break.'

'Intense, hey?' he asked, holding her gaze...intensely, he supposed.

'Uh-huh,' she said, and she gazed intensely right back.

It started as a quasi-staring competition, an almost flirtatious game, as they waited for who would blink first. But soon, it wasn't faux emerald eyes he was seeing but a memory of eyes that were big, cute, with pale blonde lashes—and brown. Deepest brown.

Eyes that had watched him, gazed at him—*needed* him.

Eyes that had scared him then, scared him with an emotion he'd recognised but knew he couldn't handle.

Eyes that had added weight to shoulders already heavy. That had tightened the invisible shackles at his wrists.

Eyes he'd *had* to walk away from.

A memory of eyes that now filled him with guilt.

Now it was easy to look away—to look anywhere but at Ella.

He stood up, the urge to move undeniable.

He hated this office; it was suffocating. He should go for a walk. Clear his head.

'Jake?'

He walked towards the door. 'Thanks for the demonstration,

Ella. I'm suitably convinced. Talk to Kerry at the front desk on your way out to book some time in my diary.'

It would be smarter to do what he'd originally intended. To tell Ella her services were unnecessary and walk away. Again.

But he couldn't do it.

What was he doing? What did he want to achieve?

'That's great,' she said, her voice rich with confusion. 'But don't you want me to go through my programme with you, so you know what to expect?'

No, not a walk. He'd go work from home. There he'd have enough space to think, to process what the hell he was doing here, with this campaign and with Ella.

Ella had spoken again, but he wasn't paying attention. So he just nodded. 'Send anything to Kerry. She can answer your questions.'

'Okay,' she said, sliding the camera back into its bag and tucking her notepad into her handbag. She crossed the room in easy, confident strides—she was fully in Ella-the-professional mode. Which was good. This version he could deal with. This version didn't remind him of a girl in a school uniform stained with tears.

'And I don't wear suits,' he said, suddenly.

'But—'

'No suits, or no programme.'

Stiffly, she nodded.

'Thanks for your time,' she said at the doorway. 'I'm really looking forward to working with you.'

Her words were mechanical.

His mind already a million miles away, he might have mumbled some form of goodbye.

And then he shut the door behind her as she left.

CHAPTER FOUR

FIRST thing Monday morning Jake stood beside the glass doors of a very exclusive Sydney salon, his shoulders propped against the stone walls of the building, both his arms and feet crossed. Jake knew the salon was exclusive as it was quite literally printed beneath the salon name above the door—personally, he felt this might bring its exclusivity somewhat into question—and his arms were crossed as it was cold.

And also, because he wasn't exactly thrilled to be here. For the zillionth time he had to ask himself exactly why he was doing this. Sure, Ella had convinced him he *might* need a little help with his image. But that help certainly hadn't needed to come from Eleanor Cartwright.

He was far from au fait with the image consultancy business, but he was pretty sure Ella didn't have a monopoly of the Sydney market.

Yet here he was. He'd made his bed, and now he'd have to lie in it.

So, right now he was considering the upcoming 'Jake Donner Rebranding Programme'—the name alone was enough to make him shudder—a little like his yearly dental check-up.

Necessary, but certainly an experience to be endured rather than enjoyed.

As he waited for Ella he observed the steady wave of commuters sweeping up Martin Place before him. Like lemmings, they moved in unison: their heads down and stride brisk. Each was barely indistinguishable from the other in their uniforms of starched shirts, dry-clean-only jackets and shiny shoes. Only the occasional loitering tourist bobbed up amongst the ocean of suits and ties to snap photos of the towering skyscrapers—oblivious to the surrounding ebb and flow of corporate Sydney.

Jake's gaze was caught by a flash of bright red amongst the crowd, and moments later Ella emerged, the colour of her scarf—neatly tucked into a long cream-coloured coat—a lonely splash of vibrancy in the grey and wintry landscape.

She walked towards him with an efficiently sexy stride. Like everyone in Sydney, she walked fast, but she managed to incorporate a gentle sway to her hips that caught his attention—and held it.

Did she have any idea how good she looked when she walked?

A second later he realised the obvious—yes, of course she did. Everything about Ella was carefully manufactured to convey and achieve exactly the image she wanted. She'd based her whole career on it.

'Good morning,' she said, ultra politely, as she came to a stop in front of him.

He nodded, and his arms remained crossed. 'Morning,' he managed, sounding about as apathetic as he felt.

She didn't even blink. 'You'll just adore Andres,' she said, ignoring his lack of enthusiasm, and the relative likelihood that he was the type of guy to 'adore' anyone—particularly hair stylists. 'What he can't do with a pair of scissors isn't worth knowing.'

He remained silent.

'You know,' she said, stepping a little closer and looking him dead in the eye, 'this isn't Chinese water torture. It's a haircut. You'll be fine.'

'I'm not worried about the haircut,' he said.

She raised her eyebrows.

'I don't like being told what to do, that's all.'

'I know that,' she said, then added quickly, 'Cynthia was very detailed in her background information.'

Ah. So she wasn't about to admit it was because she knew him so well having spent nearly every day with him for four years, then.

'I trust Andres with all my male clients,' Ella continued. 'He'll have a chat with you, find out what you like, and away you go.'

'You don't have my new haircut all picked out?' he asked, surprised.

She shook her head. 'He's the hair stylist, not me. He knows the overall look I'm after, and I trust him not to stick a bowl on your head and just trim around the edges.'

Despite himself, he hid a grin.

They headed into the salon, where Ella was greeted with a flurry of welcomes from a small army of people—many with different variations of slightly odd hair. Multicoloured, spiked bits and so on. Fortunately, Andres' haircut was more sedate, and so Jake let himself be led to a mirror, and then spent five minutes discussing his hair. Which added five minutes to the entire period of time he'd spent considering his hair, in his life.

Judging from Andres' exclamations, this lack of attention was rather noticeable. Jake didn't really get it, although he supposed, looking at himself in the mirror, maybe his hair had got slightly long. But otherwise, surely a haircut was a haircut?

Also in the mirror, Jake could see Ella chatting away to a small group of women. Amongst the chaos of the busy salon, she looked relaxed and confident. She smiled and talked with her hands, and generally just looked as if she fitted in effortlessly.

Watching her, Jake was not entirely surprised to find himself silently cheering for teenage Eleanor. Never again would she slink across a quadrangle, shoulders slumped, in an attempt to make herself as small and insignificant as possible. *Ella* would stomp her stilettos all over the girls who had bullied her so mercilessly. No one would ever guess that she was once the shy and awkward new girl at school that his fourteen-year-old self had, against his better judgment, decided to help…

Finally, he found her. She sat with her back against the corrugated iron wall of the bike shed, her knees pulled up to her chest.

'Are you okay?'

Eleanor glanced up, her face partly obscured by the tangle of her hair. But even so, Jake couldn't miss the red rims to her eyes, or the tears that had left damp patches on the chequered fabric of her school dress.

'Go away,' she said. She shifted slightly, turning her back to him.

He ignored her dismissal, instead casually dropping his back-pack onto the grass and sitting down beside her, his back to the wall, his legs stretched out long before him. It was February—the first week of school—and stinking hot, so he was wearing the awful dark grey shorts that were part of the South Beach College uniform. Mosquito bites from his walk home from school the night before patterned his legs.

Eleanor crept a little further away from him, but didn't go to leave.

'You've moved in next door to me, right?' he asked.

Even with her back to him, Jake was pretty sure she nodded.

'I only moved here last year myself.'

She remained silent.

'It's tough being new. Hard to make friends.'

'You better not try and give me advice,' she said. 'I know you don't have any friends.'

She wasn't being nasty—she was just stating the truth.

'I just don't think there's anyone at this school worth being friends with.'

'Right,' she said. 'Whatever. Can you go now?'

'Do you really want to be friends with those girls?'

Jake was pretty sure she did. He'd found himself watching her during the last couple of lunch breaks. Bravely trying to join the cross-legged circle of girls, plopping herself onto the grass as if she belonged. Every day, her attempts had failed, and the dismissive rudeness of the girls had deteriorated.

Eleanor shrugged. 'They're cool.'

'Sure. If by cool you mean they're fake, self-obsessed, mean cows.'

She giggled. 'Not all of them.'

But all of them joined in once the taunting began. Today they'd been calling Eleanor a dirty gypsy, apparently because she'd spent her childhood travelling in a caravan with her no-madic, dreadlocked parents. The joke was that whenever Elea-nor came close, they'd hold their nose and go on about the stink.

Comedy gold. Right.

Jake stood, and Eleanor craned her neck to look up at him.

'Look, if you don't want to spend your lunches sitting behind the bicycle shed, you can come sit with me, if you want.' His voice was a little gruff, and he cleared his throat. 'You know, until you make some friends.'

She studied him carefully, and he half expected her to laugh. To make a comment about not wanting to sit with the resident nerd or something. It wouldn't have bothered him if she did—he was used to it. He couldn't give a damn what anyone thought about him. He had a plan for his life—and it didn't involve any-one from this stupid school.

He didn't even know why he'd offered; it wasn't as if he knew her, or wanted company. And he was hardly known for his car-ing and sharing nature. He basically grunted at the kids in his year; he'd discovered it was an effective mechanism to keep everyone far away. Just as he liked it.

Eventually, she nodded. 'Thank you,' she said very politely. 'That's very nice, but I'm pretty sure I'll be fine.'

'No worries,' Jake said.

And he walked away.

Exactly one week later, Eleanor slid into the chair across from him at the library, and waited patiently for him to mark his place in Programming for Visual Basic.

'You were right,' she said. 'They're a bunch of nasty cows.'

'And, *voilà!*' Andres exclaimed, silencing the buzz of the clip-pers and snapping Jake back to reality. 'All done. You like?'

Jake had barely had a moment to look at himself, when sud-denly he was surrounded by what appeared to be every person who worked in the salon—rainbow hair colours and all. And Ella.

They all looked a little stunned.

What had happened to deserve such a mass, shocked reaction? Was he bald? Had they managed to dye his hair without him noticing?

But no. He looked the same. His hair was short—way shorter than it had ever been. Not quite army buzz-cut short, but close.

It actually wasn't too bad.

So he had to ask. 'What's wrong?'

'Oh, *nothing's* wrong, honey,' said the woman from the front desk. 'Trust me.'

As a group, the women—and a couple of guys—nodded.

'You know, I always thought he was pretty nice-looking when I saw him in magazines and stuff? But wow...'

'He looks kind of like that soccer player, don't you reckon? The English one.'

'Honestly, if I'd known this is what a computer geek looked like, I—'

'Thanks for the feedback, ladies,' Ella interjected, her tone just the slightest bit sharp. 'But Jake and I really need to get a move on. Busy day, you know?'

Jake's gaze darted to his watch. They were doing fine for time, actually, but he wasn't about to point that out to Ella. Before he knew it, she'd herded him out of the door. Outside, Martin Place had reduced to a trickle of foot traffic now that the majority of Sydney was safely ensconced at their desks.

Ella had already charged up the street, heading for the Armada building.

'I think those ladies had a bit more to say,' he pointed out, his longer stride easily keeping pace with her no-nonsense walk.

Ella had fished her phone out of her handbag, and her gaze was trained on its screen as she spoke. 'I think you heard enough.'

'Maybe it would be good for my self-confidence to hear people compliment my new haircut.'

She snorted. 'You know perfectly well how good-looking you are.'

The moment Ella realised what she said was obvious, the finger she'd been using to scroll through her emails stilled instantly. So did she.

'Do I?' he asked, stopping beside her.

She tilted her chin up, catching his gaze. Her eyes revealed nothing behind those damn lenses. 'It's my role to be fully aware of how you look. Objectively, you're a very handsome man, which certainly makes my job easier.'

She might as well have been describing the attractiveness of an inanimate object for all the emotion in her tone.

Without another word, Ella charged off again.

Jake followed, easily catching up within a couple of paces.

So it turned out Ella hadn't only gained conversational skills and self-confidence in the last ten or so years.

She'd also got a hell of a lot better at hiding her emotions. The Eleanor he remembered had been an open book. But Ella—Ella was more like one of those diaries with those shiny silver padlocks.

Last week, she'd slipped up, just occasionally, in his office. Glimpses of something—the Eleanor he remembered—had made it through.

But today, that was gone. If she *were* one of those diaries, it was as if she'd gone and thrown away the key.

CHAPTER FIVE

'Absolutely not.'

Judging from Jake's expression, she might as well have asked him to sell his soul. For good measure, he crossed his arms, making him six feet two-ish of *It's Not Going To Happen.*

Calmly—outwardly, at least—Ella turned to Jake's PA, Kerry, who sat serenely behind her desk. Tellingly, she did not look at all surprised.

'Did I not provide an explanation of the wardrobe audit in the schedule I sent you?' she asked, although of course she knew she had. 'Visiting said wardrobe is kind of essential.'

Kerry shrugged. She had silver hair, rather cool winged glasses and *maybe* just the slightest hint of a grin.

'I forwarded all the attached documents to Jake. Obviously he didn't get around to perusing them.'

'No,' Jake confirmed, 'I didn't *peruse* anything that involved *my home.*'

To be honest, Ella couldn't quite get her head around why he was being so resistant. What was clear, however, was that he didn't want her anywhere near his house.

She felt more than a little offended. What did she have— the plague?

'Kerry, surely you knew I'd be unhappy about this.'

The older woman didn't blink. 'Of course. However, I hoped that once you'd started the programme, you'd loosen up a little.' She paused. 'Regardless, you were free to read Ella's detailed schedule at any time.'

Jake's jaw clenched at this undeniable truth.

'By the way, *love* the haircut. Great job.' This last bit was aimed at Ella, and she smiled in response.

'Thanks. It's quite remarkable what a good stylist—'

'*Ladies.* Can we stay on topic? The point is, I don't need a wardrobe audit.'

Quite deliberately, Ella let her gaze travel up Jake's body— from his scuffed shoes, to the jeans with two rips in them, and then the jacket that looked as if it might have had a dog or cat rub up against it, as it was covered in a fine coating of white hairs.

It was supposed to be a *professional* assessment of his dire need for a wardrobe makeover, but when she found herself studying the breadth of his chest just a little too long she realised that aim had gone a little skew-whiff.

She cleared her throat. 'You need a wardrobe audit, Jake.'

He watched her with a steady gaze and an intensity that was becoming familiar.

'For the sake of argument what exactly *is* a wardrobe audit, and why must it take place at my house?'

Ella swallowed. Fired up, Jake was quite something… intimidating, even. For the first time, Ella could imagine Jake— despite his jeans—at the head of a boardroom, commanding attention. She, for one, was finding it impossible to look away.

'It's a…a…'

Ella stopped, furious with herself.

Pull yourself together, girl!

She straightened her shoulders. 'It's a standard and essential element of my services. In order to most effectively construct your new look, I need to truly understand your current situation. So I'll come to your home, and together we'll go through your existing clothing. Generally much of my client's wardrobes need to go but I'll also identify pieces in your wardrobe that can be repurposed, saving you money and ensuring that you still feel like "you"—despite your new look.'

'So basically you want to come over to my house and go through my things?'

How did Jake make her standard vanilla wardrobe audit sound so tacky?

'We'll do it together. Ideally, my clients will try on their clothes for me, to give me an idea of their preferred outfits, what they feel looks good on them and—'

'Ah,' Jake interrupted. 'So you want to come over, look through my things, and treat me like a Ken doll you get to play dress-ups with?'

Now it was Ella's turn to get all indignant. How *dared* he?

But she kept her tone steady.

'No. I want to come to your place, and *together* we would complete a wardrobe audit. It's totally standard. My clients often comment that of all my services, it's the one they most value.'

Jake looked considerably less than impressed.

'I very rarely invite guests to my home,' he said.

So now the truth came out. What was it? Was he worried about her taking photos to sell to a tabloid or something? Calling a gossip columnist as soon as she got home?

'I'm very discreet,' Ella said. 'I've been working with Sydney's rich and famous for many years. I assure you, I take your privacy very seriously. And if my word isn't enough, I'm happy to provide references.'

It was surprisingly difficult to not say what she was *really* thinking:

Stop being a jerk and trust me. I know what I'm doing.

And also:

Jake, you know *I'd never do that to you.*

But really how could he know that? It had been a very long time.

In fact the last time one of them had blindly trusted someone, like, say when she'd offered up her heart to him on a platter— well… That hadn't worked out so great, had it?

'Why did you—?'

Ella all but slapped her hand to her lips in horror at what she'd almost said.

Why did you abandon me?

Where had that come from? And in the lobby of the Armada

development floor with Jake's PA looking on with open curiosity? What was *wrong* with her?

Who cared about what some stupid seventeen-year-old boy did a hundred years ago?

Not her.

'I would've cancelled earlier if I'd understood your plans for the rest of the morning,' Jake said, misunderstanding her. 'I apologise for the inconvenience.' He hitched his backpack a little higher on his shoulder. 'I'll read through the remainder of the schedule in detail, and will advise of any other issues I come across.'

Any other issues he came across?

'Jake, I've been employed by Armada to create your rebranding programme—your schedule was not intended to be a starting position that we'd then negotiate.'

Jake shrugged. 'I'm not moving on this. You can cut my hair, tell me what to wear, teach me how to play nice with reporters—whatever. But my private life, including my home, will not become part of this circus.'

Ella opened her mouth to argue but then snapped it shut again. There was no point. So she'd just need to salvage what she could.

'Without access to your existing wardrobe, we'll need to purchase significantly more new clothes.'

He raised his eyebrows. 'Knock yourself out. Money isn't an issue.'

'And—this is non-negotiable—when we go shopping, you'll need to try on the clothes. Without any Ken-doll quips.' She watched him steadily. 'This is my job, Jake. You need to let me do it.'

After a second or two, Jake nodded. If a bit reluctantly.

'I'll also tolerate no further changes to the schedule. If, following your review, you consider anything unacceptable, then we'll end this here.' She attempted a smile, trying to appear nonchalant. 'At the very least, you've got a new haircut out of it.'

Jake's lips twitched. 'But you'd be leaving me to look too intensely at the camera all by myself.'

'And to talk too much about boring software. While wearing faded old jeans.'

Now he smiled fully. 'No more wardrobe audits?'

Ella put a hand to her heart. 'I promise.' She couldn't resist adding, 'But you're missing out...'

Jake shook his head, but his lips were kicked up in a halfway there grin. 'Fine,' he said.

Ella tried to subtly release the breath she'd been holding. Thank goodness he hadn't called her bluff—as a bluff it most certainly had been.

She wasn't about to walk away from Jake.

But he walked away from me.

No. She wasn't to think like that. This conversation—this whole situation—was about the present, not the past.

This is a once-in-a-career opportunity.

That was what this was about. Nothing else.

'I'll see you tomorrow, right?' Jake asked.

She nodded. 'Yes, we've got a tight schedule before your first interview.'

Jake rolled his eyes. 'So Marketing keeps telling me. Honestly, I think they would've preferred a parrot as the face of Armada. At least then they could stop worrying that I won't stay "on message" in my interviews.'

The last of the sentence was muttered almost absently as he turned and headed into his office, leaving Ella and Kerry alone.

'Sorry,' Kerry said. 'Jake can be a little difficult, sometimes. And he's not really into all this image stuff, you know?'

Ella murmured in agreement. Yes, she certainly did.

Kerry sighed. 'I knew he'd be funny about the wardrobe thing, but I figured because he said you knew each other, that he'd be okay with it.'

'He told you we used to know each other?' Ella's words sounded only the slightest bit strangled.

'Yes,' Kerry said, then she smiled, her expression speculative. 'You know, I was wondering about that. He didn't give any details, and—' Kerry's phone rang. 'Sorry, I'll just have to get this.'

But Ella wasn't about to wait around.

As Kerry politely answered her call, Ella mouthed her good-byes and gave a little wave as she backed away—rapidly.

She needed to send an email.

Jake guessed he was about a kilometre from home, when it began to rain.

It was hardly a surprise. Dark and stormy clouds had been perched patiently just above the sandstone cliffs that surrounded his Blue Mountains property for hours.

Yet he'd still gone for a hike, with his dogs, without any wet weather gear whatsoever.

And to think some people thought he had a brilliant mind? If they could only see him now.

Steady sheets of water had already soaked through the thin layer of his hoodie and T-shirt, and a sharp, icy breeze whipped through the valley and bit relentlessly into his skin.

For once, his office at Armada—a room of hard edges, show-stopping views of the harbour and unopenable windows that made him feel as if he worked in a Snap Lock bag—was more appealing than this place. These hundred or so acres of total seclusion.

Of total privacy.

Given he was as wet as he was going to get, right down to his thick socks and boots, it seemed almost pointless to rush back to his house. But, his dogs—Pointers with super short coats and rather wussy dispositions—had already made it clear what they wanted by shoving their bodies up hard against his legs. Albert, with his big black patches, to Jake's left, and Lizzie, with her spots and splashes of orange, to his right.

They wanted to be in front of the pot-belly stove in his lounge room.

Which didn't sound like such a bad idea at all.

Together they trekked up the gravelly path, ghost and scribbly gums lining the way. Wind gusts dislodged handfuls of fat, glossy green leaves that blew, and flew amongst the rain until they eventually fell at Jake's feet.

He hadn't planned to go so far. What had started as a quick

walk—to clear his head after his morning in the city—had, step by step, become much longer. Fortunately it had occurred to him to turn around at some point, otherwise his hot shower, and the warmth of the fire for his dogs, would be a heck of a lot further away.

This stupid campaign couldn't be over soon enough. Normally his hikes were all about his work, as, pretty much by clockwork, his mind would wander and ponder within minutes of leaving his house. Sometimes he had moments of brilliance—the sudden realisation of a solution to some coding problem; or, even better, a totally left-field idea for a new and exciting project. He needed silence and the outdoors to do his best thinking. He always had.

After all, he'd been walking home from school with Eleanor when he'd first stumbled across the idea for the online shopping cart software that launched his career and, later, Armada. She had always seemed to know when the cogs and gears in his brain started whirring at their most furious. She'd let their conversation stall, and wait, patiently, until he returned from his little mental expedition.

Then she'd listen carefully to him rabbit on about his *eureka!* moment—or, at the very least, she'd feigned interest believably.

After spending another morning with her, he wasn't any closer to understanding how much she'd changed.

And it wasn't just her appearance. Jake had checked up on her and her social life was apparently as overflowing as his was barren. Parties, openings, gala dinners—whatever—she was there.

And *that* was what he'd found himself pondering on his walk. Not something useful, like software-bug fixes or a technical proposal one of his star developers had emailed him that morning. Even memorising the sound bites he'd be required to regurgitate regularly over the next few weeks would've been a more effective use of his time.

But no. He'd just spent a good part of two hours thinking about Eleanor.

No, no. *Ella.* He couldn't forget that.

The rain had let up, just a little, and Albert and Lizzie had perked up, trotting ahead of him. Another turn and he'd be able to see his house.

Jake was attempting to look at the situation objectively.

He and Ella had been close, once. Close, angst-ridden teenagers, in fact, which had only amplified the sense of connection they'd felt. *Two against the world,* they'd been. Or rather, two against their school. The seemingly communal dislike of himself hadn't bothered Jake at all. It had been deliberate, in some ways, on his part. It wasn't as if he could ever invite a kid over to his place after school.

But he wouldn't have fitted in, anyway. Even without a mother that landed him at the end of cruel taunts, he'd been unable to comprehend quadrangle politics. He was simply happier on his own with no need to worry about saying or doing the right or cool thing. In his own little world—then as he was now—he was content.

Eleanor had been the exception. She'd been different. She'd flinched at every name she was called. At the whispers and the giggles.

But together they'd been okay. And she'd assured him she'd be fine once he'd left, that she was strong.

'I've got to go,' he said as they walked home together for the last time, his final exams only weeks away.

She slanted him a look. 'I know that,' she said simply. 'Stop worrying about me. I'll be fine.' A casual shrug. 'It's only a year. A means to an end. I'll go to school, learn, come home and then I'll be at uni before I know it. No more stupid popular groups, there.'

She was so sure.

'Then maybe one day I'll move interstate too. You can bore me to death talking about motherboards and Pascal and HTML in Melbourne, or Sydney instead—'

Then she'd shrieked when he'd glared at her, and they'd run, laughing like idiots, all the way home.

* * *

Had she been okay without him?

He'd told himself she had. Of course she had.

An image of Ella now, so perfect—so *opposite* to who she'd been—popped into his head.

Now he wasn't so sure.

The weakest rays of sunlight pushed their way through the storm clouds as Jake arrived at the foot of the staircase that led to his home. Tucked into the side of the mountain, it blended almost seamlessly into the surrounding forest. Best of all, if he was to stand on the wide verandah that edged the front of the house, he could see for kilometres. And not see another house, or another soul.

With the confidence of much experience, Lizzie and Albert thundered up the wooden stairs ahead of him. More sedately, Jake followed, each step with its own loud squelching accompaniment provided by his soaked socks and boots.

Would he have let Eleanor come to his house today?

Not Ella, but the awkward Eleanor he remembered, who wouldn't care if she got mud on her shoes or if her hair got wet in the rain?

It wasn't a sensible scenario. If Ella were still Eleanor she wouldn't be his image consultant, and she wouldn't have the urge to stick her nose into his wardrobe.

But hypothetically? Would he have classified Eleanor the same way he classified everyone else and kept her well away from this place? No one came up here any more. He had an apartment in the city he used only on occasion, and he met his few friends anywhere but here.

After Georgina had gone to the gossip magazines at the end of their relationship, he'd drawn a line in the sand.

Georgina had accused him of being closed off. Of letting nobody in.

Frankly, he couldn't see it. He had nothing inside that was necessary to share. No dark secrets—the media had mined it all. The facts were public. That was more than enough.

But, hey, if Georgina was going to have her opinion of him splashed in tawdry headlines, then he might as well live up to it.

The silence, the space, the isolation—suited him just fine.

At the top of the stairs, he walked to the balcony railing. The dogs sat patiently on the front door mat, although Lizzie gave a plaintive whine.

He looked out across the valley, past the mountains, and beyond to the very edge of the horizon.

No, not even the Eleanor he remembered belonged up here. No one did.

As he'd decided all those years ago, when he'd watched Eleanor walk across his back yard in the moonlight, her head held high and his throat choked up as he fought to stop himself calling out to her...

He was better off alone.

And Eleanor was certainly better off without him.

CHAPTER SIX

ELLA blinked, then stared at the photo in her hand. She'd torn it out of a magazine—a photo of casual leather loafers that she thought Jake could wear with jeans, but that were a significant step up from his battered sneakers. She remembered that, at least.

Why it was in her hand now—not so much.

She'd been absolutely positive she'd put the photo in her *yes* folder—the one on the ground to the left of her cross-legged knee. And yet here it was, back in her hand, the torn edges of the image rough against her fingertips.

This was getting ridiculous.

It had been nearly a week. A *week*.

At first it had made sense that she'd been a little preoccupied by Jake's unexpected, if temporary, reappearance in her life. Quite literally, her past and her—hugely improved—present had collided.

Of course she felt a little bit *off* because of it.

So when she'd stumbled occasionally at her regular salsa class, she'd been cool with it. It'd been very, very understandable.

And if the next evening—after a Jake-free day, no less—she'd found herself surrounded by her book-club girls, all looking at her expectantly and herself with no recollection of what on *earth* they were talking about... Well. That *had* been mildly irritating.

But, she'd been sure it would pass.

However by Friday, when she'd managed to forget she was meeting up with Mandy Williamson at King Street Wharf for a drink after work, she'd been *seriously* annoyed. Worse, Mandy was a past client. Ella *never* forgot anything to do with her clients.

And so now she sat cross-legged on the floor of her North Shore apartment's office-cum-spare-room, magazine clippings and images she'd printed from the Internet scattered about her like confetti.

Her iPod boomed out classic—or maybe just tragic—eighties pop music from its dock. She could never work in the total silence of Jake's building. She needed music, people, or activity, in order to function. All three was even better.

But today, even with her music, she was distracted by Jake. Again.

She had to focus.

What she was supposed to be doing was crystallising in her mind the 'look' she was trying to achieve with Jake. Given his dislike of suits, with him she had a bit of a challenge. She needed to create a wardrobe that reflected Jake—and that he would actually wear—but that was also suitable for the varied promotional events he had ahead of him. She even had a system: three manila files labeled—inventively—yes, no and maybe.

The task was taking much longer than it should.

An image of Jake, watching her with that trademark intensity kept popping into her traitorous brain.

What was it about Jake? Why did he suddenly have this power over her, when days ago he'd been little more than a forgotten memory?

Take the whole interview debacle. *She* was the one who had been so adamant that their past was irrelevant, and yet she'd still let their conversation veer in directions it should never have been allowed to go. She'd dropped her guard. And she'd done it more than once. It had to stop.

Because relaxing around Jake was dangerous. If she wasn't careful, it would be more than just echoes of their ancient friendship cluttering everything. She didn't want or *need* any reminders about their past. Her past.

As in her past she'd been Eleanor and she never wanted to be Eleanor again. To feel that way again.

Did Jake have any idea what had happened after he'd left?

She'd been outwardly so brave, encouraging him to leave, to follow his dreams. She'd seen what his mother was doing to him, the pressure he felt. The responsibility.

His scholarship had been a ticket out of a family history of poverty and underachievement. He'd had to go; she'd known it.

But then—her mum wasn't supposed to die. Her dad wasn't supposed to be lost to her in his grief.

She wasn't supposed to be left so totally and completely alone.

At school, it was as if she'd been thrown to the wolves.

Stupidly she'd reached out. Wanting friendship. Needing it desperately.

But she'd too long been classified as half of the school's 'odd couple'—an outcast. So she'd been rejected again, and laughed at, and teased. Maybe her neediness had scared them. Maybe the other girls' cruelty had stemmed from fear, or an inability to grapple with Ella's grief.

Maybe.

But she'd learnt. At university she hadn't bothered to try. She'd followed Jake's lead, needing no one.

As her dad's health had deteriorated she'd told herself she'd lost him years ago, when her mum had died. But she'd been unconvinced by her own reassurances and the depth of her pain when he was finally gone reflected the true situation.

Without him, she was left adrift. There'd been nobody and nothing in Fremantle to hold her.

So it had been absolutely the right time to reinvent herself— and she'd never, ever regretted her decision. Her life had flourished inversely proportional to how little of her old self she'd allowed to remain. It hadn't taken her long to discover that more Ella and a lot less Eleanor equalled a pretty much perfect life.

She had everything she'd always wanted.

Which was why distractions like Jake were unacceptable.

Accordingly, ten minutes wasted staring into space, and, it

turned out, unconsciously tearing a poor innocent photo of dress shoes into hundreds of tiny pieces, was totally unacceptable.

Ella leapt to her feet, scattering photos, shreds of papers, folders and Post-it notes in her wake. She slammed the door to her study, charged across her living room and burst out onto her balcony, the tiny space dappled with eucalypt-filtered light.

In the crisp winter morning's chilly freshness, she took great big swallows of air, welcoming the burn and sting to her lungs. Barefoot, she curled her toes on the freezing cement, willing the cold and the air's sharpness to knock some sense into her.

Jake was her client—nothing more.

And as he was her client, she had *no place* daydreaming about his gaze, intense or otherwise. Remnants of her schoolgirl crush on Jake Donner—next-door neighbour—had no place in her working relationship with Jake Donner—multimillionaire founder of Armada Software. This contract with Armada was the opportunity of her career and her past with Jake would not, and could not, stuff that up for her.

All she needed to do was pull herself the hell together.

Five minutes later, her mind was more appropriately—if a little forcibly—occupied with thoughts of her other clients. Six-teen-year-old Sarah who desperately need a huge dose of self-confidence leading up to her school ball. Retired teacher Joan, who was terrified she was turning into an old lady well before her time, and was desperate for an image shake-up.

Refocused, and determinedly calm, she stepped back inside.

There. It was done.

Jake equalled client.

Life equalled back to normal.

'So I was wondering,' Ella asked, standing a respectable dis-tance from Jake's changing room, 'what's the story behind you and your suit allergy? Bad experience? Unfortunate situation involving a tie?'

Jake laughed, but otherwise provided no further explanation. She stepped a little closer towards him. The menswear store's changing room had a pitifully inadequate door, so Ella could quite clearly see Jake's head and shoulders above it.

Not that she was looking or anything.

'You know, if I understand your suit prejudice, I'm in a better position to style you.'

At this, Jake stepped right up to the changing room door and shot her a bemused look. 'Right. This has nothing to do with you just being plain nosy.'

Ella shook her head primly. 'Of course not.'

He grinned, and the next thing she knew his face was obscured by his charcoal-coloured T-shirt as he whipped it over his head.

Ella took this as her cue to take a couple of big steps backwards. She didn't want to *accidentally*—of course—ogle a client.

'You know I've never given a stuff about what I wear,' Jake said, his voice a little muffled as he—it sounded like—bent over to pull on the trousers she'd picked out for him to try on.

Ella tensed at the casual reference to their once friendship. She thought she'd made herself clear in her email. Maybe he hadn't yet read it?

Although, alone in the otherwise empty change room, they were unlikely to be overheard anyway. She could relax for now.

'That doesn't mean anything,' she said. 'It took me a long time to understand the power of the right outfit. And look at me now.'

That this was a poor choice of words was immediately apparent. Jake came closer to the door again, his head tilted slightly as he made a big show of studying her. He'd shrugged on a shirt, thankfully, but he hadn't quite got around to buttoning it up. Over the door she could see a lot more bare skin than she felt was advisable.

'Hmm,' he said, just as Ella began to think that resisting the urge to fidget beneath his gaze was an impossible task. She wore a delicate cream-coloured blouse tucked into chocolate wide-leg trousers that fell perfectly over her nude patent wedges. Ella knew exactly how she looked: chic. Sophisticated. And yet the cute bow at her collar felt—suddenly—a little restrictive. She swallowed.

'Yes,' Jake finally continued, 'you obviously do give a stuff about what you wear.'

He didn't make it sound like a good thing. Or a bad thing, really.

Actually, he sounded exactly like someone who, when it came to clothes, was completely ambivalent.

Ella decided to ignore the fact that his gaze had been more *appreciative* than his words.

'It isn't really about a nice shirt or a cool pair of shoes, you know,' she said, firmly in image consultant mode. 'A person's image, and by that I mean their clothing, their grooming and their body language, has a massive impact on their lives. My clients have demonstrated that to me again and again. It's about improving self-esteem and self-confidence—and even perceptions of capability or credibility. Re-evaluating your image can be life changing.'

She definitely knew that was true.

'Yeah, yeah,' Jake said. Behind the door it looked as if he'd finally finished buttoning his shirt. 'I got all that this morning.'

He was referring to their one-hour—and one-sided—meeting in his office earlier. Ella had been fairly sure she'd been talking to herself.

'So you were paying attention?' Ella asked.

Jake swung open the changing room door as he shrugged into the soft tan leather jacket she'd selected for him. 'You lost me for a while when you started going on about colour triangles.'

'Colour *wheel,* Jake,' she said. 'I think you'll be surprised how useful it is.'

'Uh-huh,' he said as he walked a little closer to the floor to ceiling windows behind Ella.

She rolled her eyes. Jake had definitely just relegated the poor old colour wheel to his brain's recycle bin. But that was okay. It would be in Jake's Rebranding Action Plan, which she'd be handing to him in a week's time when her services ended.

She harboured some faint hope he might bother to read it, although she figured it was more likely he'd be back in his faded jeans a minute or two after the campaign concluded. And her painstakingly constructed action plan would head for a real life recycle bin. Or, more likely, a shredder.

But at least for today, and for the campaign, he was trying.

Ella propped her weight onto one heel and crossed her arms as she evaluated his outfit: tailored trousers in a muted grey-brown fabric, not too tight. A crisp off-white shirt, with a few buttons undone—definitely no tie. And a delicious leather jacket that she just adored to finish it all off.

He looked fantastic. A lot like the movie star she'd used as inspiration for all the outfits in his new wardrobe.

'What do you think?' she asked.

Jake was moving this way and that as he looked at himself in the mirror.

'Jacket's okay,' he said. 'And good call on the no-tie thing.'

But...

'Could I wear jeans instead? Not sure about these,' he said, tugging at the fabric of his trousers.

Ella sighed. How typical.

'Why?' Ella said. 'You don't like them?'

He didn't surprise her when shook his head—honestly, it was impossible to *not* like Jake Donner in those trousers. 'No, they look fine, I guess. They're just not me.'

'And we're back to the suit thing. It's denim or nothing, right?'

'I don't think nothing would go down too well on breakfast television,' Jake said with a quirk of his eyebrow, referring to the intended purpose of said trouser and leather jacket ensemble.

Ella ignored the hint of heat at her cheekbones, the sudden image of Jake wearing boxers on live TV that burnt itself into her brain, and the subsequent urge to fan herself.

'So again, I'll ask what's so bad about suits? It's like you don't understand why anyone would bother to wear one.'

'Is this a normal part of your image consulting services, Ella? Psychoanalysis?'

Ella looked up, instantly realising she was far too close, but not wanting to—literally or otherwise—back away.

'Is it so strange that I'd like to understand your clothing choices better?'

But it wasn't really just about that. She was curious and unwise, she knew. She wanted to know something more about Jake Donner the software mogul, versus the Jake she remembered.

Jake looked down at Ella. She'd ducked her head, paying a lot of attention to the lapel of his jacket, and the red in her hair shone beneath the room's down lights.

Did she have any idea what the feel of her fingers, even through the layers of leather and cotton, did to him?

She was touching him almost carelessly, as if she was going through the motions as she would any other client.

Or, more likely, it wasn't careless at all. Ella had made it clear he *was* just another client. Her really, really strange email yesterday afternoon had only underlined that.

I'd like to take the opportunity to emphasise the importance I place on my professional relationship with you, and with Armada. As discussed, our childhood friendship does not in any way impact on the delivery of my image management services. It would be appreciated if our past was kept strictly between us, as otherwise I fear my appointment as your image consultant may be misconstrued...

Yep. Definitely weird.

So her closeness was deliberate, he decided. A stubborn refusal to acknowledge that anything had once been between them.

'Well?' she said.

Today she'd forgone the blood-red lipstick, replacing it with something clear and shiny. He liked it a lot more.

'It's not a big secret,' he said, 'I did try wearing a suit, really early on when I was hunting about for venture capital and figured I needed to look like I knew what I was doing.'

And as if he could be trusted with millions of dollars, too.

'But?' she prompted.

'I hated it. The navy blue suit and tie uniform, well, it made me feel like I'd been spat out the end of a Sydney businessman assembly line.' He shrugged. 'I felt homogenised, and I didn't like it.'

Ella's forehead furrowed. 'You can be an individual in a suit,' she said. 'I dress professionally every day, but I'm not some clone. I'm still me.'

Jake searched for the words to explain. He'd never attempted to before—as he was the founder of his company, no one had ever questioned him. Without this campaign, he was positive he could've happily gone on wearing jeans to work for ever.

'I refuse to pretend to be someone I'm not,' he said. 'And I'm not someone who sees the benefit in never-ending, pointless, pontificating meetings, or long lunches full of faux camaraderie.'

'That isn't the inevitable result of wearing a suit.'

Jake shrugged. 'It's a common one. Besides, I'm a coder. People who enjoy that sort of stuff can go knock themselves out.'

That was what he was good at: coding. Of developing different ways to do things online, or using software to change the way stuff got done.

If he was having a day of naval gazing, he could probably even say that he wanted to create code that would change the way the world used technology.

If newspapers could be believed—and he knew from experience that often they could not—some people already thought he'd achieved that goal.

Yes, he acknowledged there was a purpose to meetings, and suits and suit-related duties, which was why he'd delegated the more excruciating elements of business, i.e. everything but the actual *work,* to the Armada board. He remained the founder of Armada, of course, and Director of Development. But the other stuff? He kept his toe in the water in the form of his attendance at board meetings, but that was it.

And he'd never regretted the decision—even this week. Sure, to say he was dreading the upcoming campaign would be accurate, but he'd created Armada's current corporate structure for this very reason: to ensure that people with better brains for business kept his company running, and kept his software and, with the phone, his new technologies, out there for the public to use.

That was the thrill he got out of the job.

And he didn't need a suit to achieve it.

Ella was playing with the ridiculous bow at her neck, her fingers running up and down the long pieces of silk that draped part of the way down the curve of her breasts. He knew she wasn't doing it consciously, but the action was most definitely compelling.

Before he starting thinking too much about what would happen if she pulled too hard and the bow unravelled, he backed up a step. 'I'll go try on one of the other outfits,' he said, just a little bit hoarsely.

Inside the change room, he made quick work of unbuttoning and shrugging out of his shirt.

'That sort of makes sense,' Ella said. 'A kind of eccentric sense, and I can't say I agree with it—but sense, nonetheless.'

'Thanks,' he said dryly. He hung the shirt back up on a hanger, and turned to the stack of other clothes hooked on the far wall of the change room. At the very back, behind a stack of shirts, disturbingly expensive fine wool jumpers and a heck of a lot of jackets, something caught his eye.

'Although it kind of falls down when you start talking about public appearances, like what you're about to do. Or other occasions to wear a suit. Like weddings. Or...'

'The Armada phone launch party,' he finished. Jake pulled the offending item from its hook.

'I guess you found the suit—'

Ella went silent when he threw open the change-room door and held the jet-black suit jacket and trousers out in front of him.

'You're not wearing a shirt,' she said, pointing out the obvious in a small voice. Her gaze rocketed about the room before settling very firmly on his face.

'I'm also not going to wear a suit, Ella.'

'You have to wear a suit to the launch party. The dress code's cocktail.'

He shook his head. 'No way.'

Her eyes narrowed. 'Now you're just being stubborn.'

He supposed he was. He'd attended weddings before. And worn a suit, even. His ex had bought the one he'd worn to the last wedding he'd attended, actually.

But that wasn't the point.

'It was the one thing I made *very* clear when I agreed to all of this.'

He'd been independent his *whole* life. His parents certainly hadn't provided any guidance. None of his girlfriends had had any success when they'd tried.

He did his own thing. Made his own decisions.

Being told what to wear was bad enough. He'd needed to be the one to set the boundaries to at least have that control.

'You agreed to follow my programme,' Ella said, every line of her body tense and verging on combative. 'To let me do my job. If I let you rock up at the awards night in jeans and sneakers, I'll be a laughing stock. So will you.'

She snatched the coat hanger out of his hands.

'I didn't just grab any old suit, Jake. There's no tie, for one, and the cut is exceptional. You'll be amazed how comfortable it is.'

In response, Jake just shook his head.

Ella shook the hanger a little as her frustration seeped out. 'Trust me, and just try the damn thing on. You're being an idiot about this.'

'Is that how you normally talk to your clients?' he asked.

Ella went perfectly still.

A beat later, he watched as she deliberately rolled her shoulders back. Then she calmly lay the suit over her arm, smoothing it into place.

'My apologies,' she said, in a totally different voice from before. 'I've handled this very badly. I'd hate for you to be in any way uncomfortable at the launch, and I'm concerned if you're inappropriately dressed you'll regret your decision. Would it help if—?'

'Stop,' Jake said. 'Don't do the whole pretending-you-don't-know-me nonsense again, Ella. I don't want to hear it.'

She sucked in a breath. 'I thought I made it very clear in my email. It's best if we start afresh. We're obviously both different people.'

'That was a nice idea, Ella. But that's not the first time you've called me an idiot, and it's stupid to pretend that it is,' he said, referring to their many fights as teenagers. Usually over topics like the best buses to catch to get to the beach, or whether the movie *Dirty Dancing* could acceptably be referred to as a 'classic'. Ella had thought so. Jake—immovably—did not.

At the worst possible time, a man walked into the change room. He glanced momentarily at Ella and Jake, seemed completely unbothered by the sight of a half naked man and an obviously irate woman, and disappeared into the cubicle three doors to their left.

'I would really prefer it if you didn't talk about our past,' she said, in a fierce stage whisper. She marched past him into his change room. 'Can you come in here, please?'

He followed her, and when he pulled the door shut behind him, automatically turning the dial to mark the room as occupied, the space was suddenly intimate. The mirrors that near covered three walls of the tiny room reflected them from nearly every angle.

Jake had the completely inappropriate realisation that now he had a really fantastic view of Ella's butt.

She put her hands on her hips, and he dragged his eyes back to her, and not to the view so generously offered by the mirror.

'I'm sorry,' he said suddenly, shocking himself. Where had that come from?

Ella looked equally gobsmacked, her mouth forming a perfect O.

For a few minutes they just stood there, blinking at each other. *What was he sorry for? Ogling her? Not trying on the suit?*

'About how I left. About how I didn't stay in touch,' he clarified—both for himself and Ella. 'Is that what this is about?'

'Of course not,' she said, still in that ridiculous whisper. Who gave a crap if a total stranger three doors down heard them? 'Nothing has anything to do with that.'

The edge to her tone proved the opposite was true.

'I'm not proud of myself,' he said. 'I thought it was better to have a clean break. Let us both start afresh.'

The explanation sounded as pathetic as he now thought it was. At the time, it had seemed the only solution. Noble, even.

But it hadn't been about that, not at all. She'd desperately wanted him to stay. Needed him to stay—and to love her.

Both had been impossible.

'You've got nothing to apologise for. I was totally, totally fine.'

He'd told himself that, too. She was strong. And she'd had her dad who loved her, and would support her.

He couldn't have offered her either.

'I'm sorry,' he said again, because it seemed the only thing worth saying.

How to put thirteen years of absence into words? He hadn't been noble. He'd been scared.

'After I lost Mum,' Ella said, 'it hurt more than I could ever, ever describe in words. It left a hole, you know? And then you left, too...'

Her bottom lip quivered, and emotion hummed in the small room. Part of him was glad she'd dropped the act, but then *this* was why he'd left. This depth of emotion. This loss, this grief.

He couldn't process it. He didn't understand it.

Not then, and not now.

At seventeen, he couldn't handle it. At thirty he couldn't either. He felt useless, helpless.

So he did the only thing he could—with utterly no idea if it would help or hinder—and he reached for her.

The space was so small that with one stride he was before her, and a moment later his arms encircled her.

It should've been awkward, and it was, at first.

Ella gasped at his touch and stiffened. But almost instantly her body softened, and she leant into him. And then it felt like the most natural thing in the world.

Against his bare chest, she felt the wetness of her cheeks.

For a really, really long time, they just stood there, Jake watching his hands rub rhythmically up and down her back in the mirror as her body shook, ever so slightly.

Then, after an age, she turned her face up to him.

'You shouldn't have disappeared,' she said.

In this moment, looking down at her, her mascara smudged, and strands of her long hair rubbed loose and framing her eyes haphazardly, he agreed with her.

I should've kissed you.

Did she guess what he was thinking? Maybe, because something changed in their embrace. His shirtless state—minutes ago so irrelevant—now only added to the charged atmosphere. He suddenly registered the bite of her nails as they trailed down his spine.

Then she licked her lips, and he was lost.

His arms tightened, and he leant towards her. She moved too, close enough that he felt her breathing, quick and shallow, against his lips

But then she was gone.

She bumped against the mirror behind her in her urgent retreat.

'Thank you for the apology,' she said. 'Appreciate it.'

Her voice was that faux professional one, and she was using it, as always, to put distance between them.

Which certainly wasn't a bad idea. His brain still felt fuzzy. His body definitely still wanted to reach for her. To kiss her.

So distance was good. Necessary.

'So you'll try on the suit?' she asked.

The question was so incongruous, he had to laugh. 'Seriously?'

Her lips curled upwards, although she still had a telltale sheen to her eyes. 'I reckon it's the least you can do.'

He nodded. And he knew he'd be wearing the damn thing to the launch, too.

Ella managed a brief, victorious smile. But then her expression morphed abruptly back to deadly serious.

'This doesn't change anything, though. I still stand by what I said in that email. Please don't let on to anyone that we knew each other. Or even that I lived in Fremantle. Definitely don't say anything about my...' she took a deep breath '...my mum, either. Okay?'

After what had just happened—and what had happened all those years ago—he wasn't about to deny her this. He nodded.

'But why? Surely your friends and clients know you're from Fremantle? And what school you went to? It wouldn't be that hard to figure out you used to know me.'

She shook her head, the action verging on violent.

'No. No one knows.'

'Where you're from?' he asked, confused. Why would she hide that?

'Exactly. And that's how it's going to stay.'

CHAPTER SEVEN

I REFUSE *to pretend to be someone I'm not.*

Jake's words most unexpectedly popped into Ella's head as she stared at herself in the mirror.

It shouldn't have surprised her, really. Their whole conversation had crowded most of the space in her brain ever since the not-soon-enough conclusion to Jake's personal shopping expedition.

This was why Jake was supposed to have remained at a distance, safe beyond the protective barrier of professionalism.

She'd attempted a couple of different approaches to dealing with the events of the day. The first approach had been sound in theory: the She Was Glad It Happened approach. This was based on the idea that they'd 'cleared the air', and now could proceed along an obstacle-free path—two adults with no unanswered questions between them.

Unfortunately this theory short-circuited whenever she remembered the exact moment Jake had decided to kiss her. And that she'd decided to kiss him back.

What on earth had she been thinking? This was the man that had hurt her *so much.* Who had abandoned her when she'd needed him the most.

Thankfully—*thankfully*—she'd come to her senses.

But still, she'd cried in his arms even before her hormones had taken control. When was the last time she'd let someone see her cry? She couldn't remember.

She couldn't even be sure why she'd cried.

So no, she definitely couldn't be glad it had happened.

This had led neatly to her next plan of attack: Pretend It *Never* Happened.

Ella was confident that this was the better approach. She only had another week or so scheduled with Jake, and then she could move on with her life, exactly as it had been before he'd burst back into it.

Occasional unfortunate flashbacks to how good he'd looked without a shirt, notwithstanding.

Yes. It was a good theory.

So she'd organised impromptu drinks with a couple of girlfriends even though it was a Tuesday night. What better way to move on than a reminder of exactly how far she'd come?

I refuse to pretend to be someone I'm not.

Ella shook her head, as if she could physically dislodge the echo of Jake's words.

She needed to focus. She had to leave in a few minutes.

She deliberately twisted her body this way and that, on the lookout for even the smallest flaw in need of correction. Her gaze travelled from her carefully straightened hair, to her midnight-blue dress and the less than extravagant curves it showcased. Her skin glowed—the result of regular spray tans—and her pedicured toes were encased in super strappy faux snakeskin heels.

Ella stepped closer to the mirror, near enough to evaluate the carefully applied liquid eyeliner, the curled and mascara-ed eyelashes, the expertly blended smokiness of her eye shadow. Her teeth were straight, and white. Her eyebrows the ideal shape. Her irises a shade of green that 'popped' against the undertones of auburn in her hair.

She looked—perfect.

Not perfect in a supermodel way, but perfect in the-very-best-version-of-Ella way. Picture perfect, just as her business name promised.

Normally such an assessment would make her feel good. After all, she worked damn hard to maintain this 'look' for every occasion. It certainly didn't come easily for her.

However, tonight, Jake had ruined it. Tonight, for the first time since she'd transformed herself all those years ago, doubt niggled.

As she watched her lips thinned.

No. No way. She was not going to let Jake get to her.

And so she grabbed her handbag, her jacket, and headed back into the city.

Unfortunately, it was obvious, almost immediately, that the Pretend It Never Happened theory was easier said than done.

At a bar in King Street Wharf, she barely managed to follow the conversations of her friends.

'You okay?' Mandy asked, her blue eyes wide with concern. 'It's not like you to be so quiet.'

Sharon, her long black hair still managing to shine in the trendy shadows of the bar, wore a matching worried expression.

'Of course!' she replied, because what else could she say? She hadn't exaggerated when she'd told Jake that no one in Sydney knew of her past.

She hadn't lied, as such, more *omitted* details.

Surprisingly, it wasn't all that difficult to do so if you conducted your social life primarily at parties, bars and nightclubs. Friendships based around shouted conversations, consumption of many cocktails and questionable dancing were necessarily maintained at a rather superficial level.

When she'd moved to Sydney, she'd been desperate for a life in stark contrast to the one she'd always known. Where she'd once been alone she wanted to be surrounded by crowds and vibrancy; where she'd once had a life full of loss and sadness, she'd searched for fun and gloss and nothing too serious.

But today she wanted more.

How could that be possible? She had everything she'd always wanted.

Rather than think about that, she headed for the bar. She thought she might have said something to her friends, but she couldn't be absolutely sure.

The bar was crowded, three or four people deep, but she made a beeline in its direction. She needed a drink.

Normally she loved the buzz of Sydney's night life. She loved the music, loved the dancing, loved the type of silly conversation people tended to have when they'd had more than a cocktail or two. All dressed up and out with her girlfriends, she could laugh and dance with them, or laugh and dance with total strangers. She could do anything. Forget herself. Be anyone.

Wait. Not anyone. She could be *Ella.*

Ella was who she wanted to be. She loved her life. Was proud of how far she'd come, and who she'd become.

A barman was speaking to her, and, judging from his expression, not for the first time. 'What can I get you?' he asked, his voice loud in order to be heard over the beat of the music.

Ella shook her head. She didn't want a drink any more. She wanted to be alone.

She walked back to Sharon and Mandy, gave a half-hearted explanation for leaving, and then was gone before they had a chance to ask any questions. She wound through the crowd that packed the nightclub, picked up her jacket from the cloakroom, and then burst out into the street, the cool night air a welcome relief to her suddenly hot and terribly uncomfortable skin.

A short taxi ride later, and back in her lounge room, she went to dock her iPod, the movement automatic after years of repetition. But her hand stilled as she wrapped her fingers around the device's hard edges.

Instead she dropped her bag to the ground and flopped herself onto her sofa. For once she wanted to be in the quiet.

She needed to think. Needed to reshuffle her thoughts, just a little. Reassure herself.

She believed, completely, in what she taught her clients. She believed everything she'd told Jake about the power of personal appearance, despite his obvious scepticism.

He wasn't the first person in her life who'd believed that appearance didn't matter. Far from it.

Who cares what anyone else thinks, Eleanor? We love you and anyone who doesn't is plain silly. You're perfect just as you are.

Yep. Just as she was. Bad hair, unfashionable clothes and all.

Her parents had meant well—but they'd been so, so misguided.

But she'd started off believing them, of course. Why wouldn't she? Her mum with her crazy, home-made clothes, always in vibrant, textured fabrics—like lush purples, or metallic golds, or emerald greens. And then her dad, with his mad bohemian dreadlocks, strong opinions, loud voice and never-wavering love. Together they'd been a force of nature—impossible to ignore.

But then her mum was gone, and Ella realised they'd been wrong. She'd been wrong.

Because of course it mattered.

There was no point pretending she didn't care what anyone else thought, if being herself—just as her mum had said—left her alone. Everyone needed someone.

As her dad had *needed* her mum. So badly that he'd never been the same since Valerie Cartwright had stepped out onto that street without looking. Ella'd always thought she'd probably been daydreaming; off in her own little fantasy world, and quite simply forgotten to check for oncoming traffic.

The end result was a husband and father left rudderless. Overcome by grief that he never, ever recovered from. To the point where Ella was convinced that even though it took four long years he truly did die from a broken heart.

And a heart that had been too broken to have space for Ella.

But with Jake long gone, he'd been all she'd had. Then he was gone too, and she'd been truly alone.

No longer was it okay to say *I don't care what anyone else thinks,* because, quite frankly, being alone sucked.

Which was why Eleanor Cartwright had re-invented herself. From a place of grief she'd created something *good.* Something *better* than before.

She'd never looked back.

At some point Ella had closed her eyes, but now she opened them, staring up at her stark white ceiling and the rice paper light shade almost directly above her head.

The silence wasn't soothing any more. It was just…empty.

Within a minute she had her iPod in place and music on—loudly.

Loud enough to flow through to every nook and cranny of her house.

And loud enough to muffle and blur even the slightest whisper of doubt.

CHAPTER EIGHT

JAKE was sitting in the studio of a commercial radio station—not fidgeting.

Although it was taking some effort.

Through the glass walls, he could see Ella, her legs crossed elegantly, immaculate and serene in her tweed suit with over-sized black buttons. If she was at all worried about how he was about to go in his very first interview for the Armada campaign, she hid it well.

If she'd been in any way impacted by their impromptu rendezvous in that change room, she hid that even better. It'd been almost a week, and her veneer of professional perfection had produced not the tiniest fissure.

It went without saying that he'd enthusiastically followed her lead.

When he caught her gaze, she smiled encouragingly, then mouthed: *You'll be fine.*

He wasn't nervous, as such.

More…tense.

Even after more than a week of preparation with Ella and with Armada's board and marketing departments his level of interest in the task at hand had not demonstrably increased. He still didn't like the media. He still didn't like the idea of primping and preening and pretending.

But he was, inarguably, ready for this.

He'd been groomed, and dressed and coached within an inch of his life.

'Today we have Jake Donner, founder of Armada Software, visiting us here on Drive 97.2FM. Listeners may remember Jake as the boy-wonder programmer who took the online world by storm in the late nineties, but who has more recently become famous as Sydney's most mysterious billionaire bachelor.'

Jake cringed inwardly at the presenter's choice of words. Mysterious? Really?

He was a computer geek with a low tolerance for those that pried into his private life. No mystery there!

'Jake's here today to talk about his company's latest venture into the crowded smart-phone market. And I'm hoping we'll get to learn a little more about the mystery man as well. Jake Donner—thanks for joining us today.'

Jake nodded, then realised he needed to actually talk. 'Good morning, Nick, it's great to be here.'

A few seconds later, given the time delay beyond the sound-proof studio, Ella grinned and gave a thumbs-up sign. He was on his way.

After a few questions, none curly, Jake was getting into the swing of things. He even cracked a smile at one of the presenter's halfway humorous jokes. He felt the tension in his back and shoulders ease, and he settled more comfortably into his chair. He even had the thought that he might ask the producer, currently sitting across from him and fiddling with various dials and buttons while the interview took place, a few questions about how all the technology worked, after the show.

This isn't so bad.

'Okay, Jake—enough about the phone. Let's get onto the questions our listeners really want the answers to.'

Even this didn't rebunch his muscles. He was ready for this. Ella had taught him strategies to deal with anything he didn't want to answer. It was simple: Deflection, Distraction, Decoy or Denial.

'Three years ago you applied a strict no-interview policy following the highly publicised breakup between yourself and Georgina McAvoy, who has since become one of Sydney's most photographed socialites.'

Jake had never fully understood how it was possible to make a career out of being someone's ex but, somehow, Georgina had managed it.

'But here you are today, pushing the new Armada phone. And I hear you have quite an aggressive promotional schedule ahead of you. What's changed?'

'Well, I think it's important to mention that there was never a formal no-interview policy.' He shrugged. 'I figured Georgina was doing—and continues to do—enough talking for the both of us.'

The presenter laughed.

'But more seriously, I value my privacy, and keeping a low profile remains extremely important to me. So you can take the fact I'm here today as a clear reflection of how much I believe in this product. This phone will revolutionise smart-phone technology, and I'm prepared to step outside of my own comfort zone to communicate that to people.'

Yep. That was far more effective then *Armada had no other option.* Or—*it's none of anyone's business why I choose to do anything, Nick*—which would have been on the tip of his tongue a couple of weeks ago.

'Right, right,' the presenter said, nodding. 'Now, I've got to ask this, now we've mentioned Georgina. Is Sydney's most eligible bachelor seeing anyone at the moment?'

He was ready for this too. 'No,' he said with a smile. 'I'll be attending the Armada phone launch tomorrow night without a plus one. And, Nick, I can't say how much I'm looking forward to introducing this phone to the Australian public. Australia— and the world—hasn't seen anything quite like it.'

Through the glass, Ella beamed at him, and Jake had to admit he felt a little smug.

The last time a reporter had asked him about his relationship status he'd as good as bitten their head off—*and* consequently ended up on the front page of the paper looking like a close relation to the devil incarnate. It was how he'd discovered his glare was more effective than he'd ever imagined.

So—this was a huge improvement. He was the one in charge. And even on message.

He shoots...he scores!

The presenter, however, looked less than impressed. He must have expected a scoop. Fireworks. Anger. Simmering silence—*anything.*

And Jake was not going to give him what he wanted.

He met the guy's frustrated gaze with one that was steady and in control.

You're getting nothing from me, mate.

But then, the presenter's eyes gained a calculating glint.

'I hear you moved your mother from Fremantle to a nursing home close to your estate in the Blue Mountains some months ago. Just how is she finding life in New South Wales?'

Instantly, Jake tensed. From the top of his newly styled hair to the soles of his funky distressed leather loafers.

This was the one—the one—topic that Jake had made clear was off limits. He had no doubt that this had clearly been communicated to the slimy presenter sitting no more than a metre away from him.

The presenter's eyes darted downwards, and Jake made himself relax the fingers he hadn't even realised he'd formed into fists.

The other man was tall, but soft. Easy pickings for a man who didn't just hike through the mountains that surrounded his home—but climbed them.

But that, of course, was exactly what the guy wanted. By asking that question he'd just instantly cancelled all Armada advertising contracts at the radio station indefinitely—so he was betting on a newsworthy reaction. He'd like nothing more than for Jake to do exactly what he very badly wanted to do.

But Jake would not give him that pleasure.

'I'm told she is doing very well,' he said, managing to force the words through his teeth.

'Told?' the slime asked, feigning ignorance. 'You haven't visited her?'

Jake's jaw clenched and unclenched. He should probably be

taking slow, deep breaths or something. Or spouting some Armada-approved sound bite.

But he couldn't do it. He had no intention of explaining anything to do with the woman whom he'd housed since he was eighteen years old, whom he'd financed through round after round of treatment at Australian and international rehabilitation clinics that had promised the world—only to produce a woman who relapsed within weeks. Months if he was lucky.

The more he'd done for her, the more her resentment had grown.

Until finally, after a lifetime of self-abuse, she'd lost her mind.

Through the glass wall, Jake could see Ella stand up, and walk right up close. He expected her to be shaking her head, or glaring at him, or holding her hands up in a big STOP motion.

She was doing none of those things.

In fact, her hands were on her hips, her nostrils were flared, and her cheeks flamed pink. She looked about as furious as he felt. Like if it were possible for her to somehow teleport herself through that glass barrier, then slimy Nick the radio presenter would be in very, very serious trouble.

A sudden image of Ella, in her knee-high boots and elegant little suit, socking that guy in the nose, sprang fully formed to his mind.

It made him smile.

This unexpected turn of events clearly threw dear old Nick. 'Jake?' he asked, his eyes wide.

'No comment,' he said, utterly polite. 'My family is off limits. No exceptions.'

A pause, and Nick's gaze was no less calculating.

'A source at the nursing home reports that your mother has been asking for you…'

Okay. Ella as his knight in shining armour or not, he'd reached his limit.

He couldn't trust himself to speak, because nothing he would say would even vaguely resemble an Armada approved sound bite—or anything acceptable for a daytime radio audience. Not by a long shot.

He stood, without a word. Turned, and headed towards the door.

The slimy piece of scum gleefully reported Jake's progress to his audience of probably hundreds of thousands. Jake didn't care. He wanted out of here.

But at the door, he paused. Then, very deliberately, walked back to the desk.

The other man recoiled, which was semi satisfying.

Although Jake ignored him.

Instead, he leant forward, and said—very calmly, and very clearly—into the microphone, the following:

'Go to hell.'

Ah. Yes. That hit the spot.

Together, Jake and Ella exited the radio station in a very mature and unhurried manner, while maintaining a dignified silence.

This lasted for approximately ten metres once they'd burst out onto the busy Pyrmont street. Jake grabbed Ella's hand and tugged her down a narrow side road, where, for a few moments, they stared at each other. Trying not to laugh.

And failed.

It started off slow, with little bursts of mirth. But soon, it descended into totally-lost-it fits of gasping and tear-inducing laughter.

'Why are we laughing?' Jake asked, after an age.

Ella, hugging herself in a partially successful attempt to contain her still continuing giggles, was at a loss. 'I have no idea. You should be furious, actually.'

'I know,' he said, tilting his head as if in contemplation. 'I was.'

Inexplicably, this started Ella off again. 'I noticed.' Then added in little gaspy breaths. 'You were...very...very...angry.'

He smiled—a huge wide smile that she hadn't seen in years. 'So were you. If you'd got your hands on him you would've got him good,' he teased.

'I would've!' she said, and meant it. Honestly, she'd been on the verge of tearing that awful radio presenter limb from limb.

Familiar pain had etched itself in every line of Jake's face as soon as his mother was mentioned—and in the moment she'd hated that man for doing that. 'It was just that pesky wall in the way.'

'Yeah,' Jake said, nodding sagely. 'Walls can be so inconvenient.'

Coming from Jake, that inanity was all the more ridiculous, and the laughter began afresh.

Slowly, slowly, reality reimposed itself. Ella knew it was all kinds of wrong for her to approve of what had just happened.

What she should be doing was a formal debrief. First, she should highlight the positives—and there were many. For ninety per cent of the interview, Jake had been near unrecognisable with no sign of the surly, reclusive billionaire.

And then she should cover the areas for improvement. Armada would certainly expect her to. She should be implementing future strategies to avoid such a circumstance happening ever again.

'That was awesome,' she said, instead.

He knew exactly what she meant.

'I shouldn't have done it.'

Ella nodded. 'We both know that. But I'm still glad you did. He deserved it.'

They shared a different smile then. Something softer, and more subtle. For the first time since those minutes in that change room, Ella let her gaze lock for long moments with his.

'He wasn't supposed to ask me about my mum.'

'Some journalists only care about the story,' she said.

Jake rubbed his forehead. 'And I gave him one.'

'I still think you did the right thing.'

Continuing to hold her gaze, he spoke more quietly. 'Are you saying that as Ella Cartwright, Image Consultant and Rebranding Guru, or as the girl who used to be my next-door neighbour?'

She should be annoyed he was doing this, bringing up their past. She should also be annoyed he told someone to *go to hell* on live radio. And at herself for standing in a public street, laughing like a loon with a client.

But of course, she was annoyed at none of those things.

'I know how much your mum hurt you,' she said. 'I remember.'

Jake held up a hand, ticking items off with a finger. 'Yeah, like remembering finding her passed out on my kitchen floor. Or screaming at you like a banshee when she thought you'd stolen her precious pills. Or never being proud when I got straight As...'

He dragged his gaze from hers, and directed it at the overcast sky.

'She's lucky to have you.'

Jake shook his head, still not looking at her. 'She hates me, you know,' he said.

'Oh, Jake, I'm sure she doesn't.'

Ella said the words automatically, but had no idea if they were true.

'Growing up, she always said she loved me. Remember?'

Ella nodded. It was as if, in the short periods of time that Diana Donner had emerged from her drug-muddled haze, the woman had thought that saying *You know I love you so much, Jake, right?* somehow made it all okay.

She'd said it all the time, proudly, and maybe even deliberately in front of Ella. As if she had something to prove. Which, Ella supposed, she did. She'd wanted to prove she was a decent mother.

Obviously, on absolutely every level, she'd failed.

But of her most spectacular motherly failure, Jake had never spoken to Ella about. The incident at the school assembly—complete with bathrobe and shrieking proclamations of love. It was before Ella had started at South Beach College, but the story had become school quadrangle legend. So she knew.

'But you don't hate her?' Ella asked, guessing.

His chin dropped down until he was looking at Ella dead on. 'No,' he said, simply.

Now they stood together, most definitely not laughing. Memories seemed to cloak them. Not just of Jake's mum, either.

How many times before had they walked together down a quiet street? Hundreds? Thousands? There'd been so many long conversations—some full of laughter, some not at all—as they'd walked to and from school. Except for when Jake went off on one of his exploratory mental tangents, and then she'd known to stay perfectly silent.

Then there was the giggling side by side in front of the TV as they'd watched comedies they'd taped onto VHS. And the hours spent together at the library during lunch breaks, happily conforming to the geeky stereotype that'd been applied to them. But Ella had been no semi-genius like Jake—she'd just loved to read. And read.

In books, at least, the unpopular outcast always seemed to have a happy ending.

'How did you get started in this?' Jake asked, suddenly.

'In what?'

He gestured vaguely at her. 'This. Your job. Back at school, you wanted to be a librarian.'

He said it as if it'd been written in stone. Which, she guessed, it kind of had.

'That was just so I could read books all day,' she said, not all that surprised that his thoughts—his memories—had mirrored hers so closely. 'I went to uni for a few years, but then my dad got sick and, well, things changed. I changed.'

She'd had to change.

'I heard about your dad,' he said quietly. 'I'm sorry.'

'You sent flowers, I remember.' Ella swallowed. With time, it didn't really get all that much easier. 'Thank you.'

Somewhere at the back of her mind, Ella conceded that she was being quite okay about this—about this acknowledgement of their past. Of their past friendship.

'The image-consultant thing was kind of an accident,' she said, after a while. 'When Dad died, I didn't know what to do. Apart from leave Perth, definitely. I wanted to start afresh.'

'I get that,' he said.

The simple words made her smile. 'I *know* you do. You as good as counted down the days until you could leave Fremantle from about age fourteen.'

He shrugged. 'I needed to leave.'

She agreed. He did. Just, at the time, she'd never imagined he wouldn't look back.

'And I figured,' she continued, refusing to dwell at *all* on that, 'that I might as well do it properly. So before I left I did a lot of research. Some on the Internet, and I read a lot of books about dressing for your body type, using make-up, that sort of thing. By the time I landed in Sydney, I walked off the plane a whole new person.'

That she had. She'd only had the one 'Ella' outfit at the time, but she'd stepped into Sydney Domestic terminal wearing it. And she'd felt better—and stronger—than she could ever remember.

'I was so amazed at how differently people were treating me, that I wondered if somehow I could turn it into a career. Help out other sad cases like me. I worked for the original owner of Picture Perfect for a few years, and then bought the business from her when she sold it.'

'Doesn't it bother you,' Jake asked, 'how differently you're treated now?'

She knew what he was asking. He thought everyone should be treated the same, even if they wore a hessian sack and didn't know the first thing about social or professional etiquette. But life didn't work that way.

'Image is everything, Jake,' she said firmly. Then added more lightly, 'Haven't I managed to teach you anything?'

He shook his head, a very deliberate movement. Then he reached forward, the feather-light touch of his finger at the bridge of her nose sudden and completely unexpected.

Gradually, and with excruciating slowness, the pad of his forefinger traced its way down to the tip of her nose.

The action was completely inappropriate. They had a professional relationship!

But that was now a lie, and she knew it.

'I thought it was cute,' he said, with no further explanation.

He meant the bump on her nose.

Now she took a step back, swiping her hand in front of her face to bat his fingers away.

'It was *ugly*. It needed to be fixed.'

'Did you think your name was ugly too? And the colour of your eyes?'

'Yes.'

Again he shook his head. 'You were wrong.'

Frustration bubbled up inside her. How could she possibly make him understand? He saw the world in black and white; he always had.

But he was wrong, so wrong, when it came to this. She had nearly a decade of success in Sydney that proved that time and time again.

'We'll have to agree to disagree,' she said, because to say anything else would be pointless.

The atmosphere had shifted.

'Well,' Ella said briskly. If Jake had asked again, now she most definitely was speaking as Ella Cartwright, Image Consultant and Rebranding Guru, and *not* the girl next door. 'Overall, I think you did really well today. I'm so pleased with your progress.'

Jake rolled his eyes. Five minutes earlier she would have called him on it, but now their professional boundaries were firmly back in place.

'Now, tomorrow is our very last session. I bet you're glad to reach the end, hey?' She spoke with such false heartiness that she thoroughly deserved Jake's dismissal of her words.

'On networking, right?'

'Yes. Perfectly timed with the launch that evening.'

Jake pulled his phone out of his jacket pocket. The jacket was an industrial-looking piece she'd chosen for him—along with his white shirt, light grey jumper and, especially for him, designer jeans. He'd disregarded her suggestion to wear the co-ordinated scarf, but otherwise he looked perfect. Perfect enough that she was so momentarily distracted admiring him that she forget he was checking his phone for something.

'I can't make it.'

'What?' she said. Then swallowed, and tried again. 'I mean, pardon me?'

His lips quirked. And was that a cheeky sparkle in his eyes?

'Something's come up.' He slid the phone back into his pocket with an air of finality.

'Cynthia made it very clear that you required particular assistance with your networking skills.'

'I completely agree,' he said. To her surprise.

'Oh. So you want to reschedule to later in the day? I believe our meeting was scheduled for ten. I've got another meeting in the early afternoon, but I should be available around four? Although, that won't give you much time to get ready—'

'No,' he said, as if there was no room for negotiation. 'I'm busy all day.'

Flummoxed, Ella propped her hands on her hips. 'Why don't you tell me what you're getting at, Jake?'

'I require your services—to guide me in the gentle art of civil conversation—'

'Networking,' Ella interrupted.

Jake ignored her. '—during the Armada Smart Phone launch party.'

'During? You mean, have me attend?'

Jake nodded slowly, as if explaining to something rather dense.

'But I have plans,' she said. And she did. She always did.

'Can they be cancelled? It's very important to me that you're there.'

The way he was looking at her, right this instant, all intense and compelling and moody and gorgeous with his icy blue eyes…

Friday night cocktails at the Opera Bar sounded imminently cancellable.

Mutely, she nodded.

Then he was holding out his arm, a taxi was pulling in beside them, and she found herself bundled into the back seat, her handbag somehow ended up neatly on her lap. She looked up at Jake, outside the car, leaning with his arm propped against the top of the open door.

'I'll email you the invitation,' he said. Then he added, with a grin more wicked than should be allowable, 'Dress to impress. I hear the dress code's cocktail.'

CHAPTER NINE

So far, the launch party was exactly as excruciating as Jake had expected. It had it all: inane conversation. Wannabes posing all over the place. Air kisses. Overly loud laughter. An abundance of suits.

And it had only been going fifteen minutes.

He sipped on his beer, surveying the room from where he stood, braced against the bar. Armada had booked out the opulent Darling Harbour restaurant for the launch, and beyond the crowd of Armada staff members and the aforementioned wannabes large windows opened out to a balcony. The sun had long ago set on this late winter evening, so the water was just a black nothingness, reflecting the multicoloured lights of the casino that loomed above it. Jake knew this, as he'd been out there on the balcony a few minutes earlier. Unfortunately, his tolerance for pointless conversation was as low as usual, and so he'd excused himself to get a drink.

He was fully aware his time alone would not last.

He was supposed to be out there, schmoozing. Regurgitating the Armada 'mission' and 'message', just as he had on the radio yesterday. Except for the bit at the end, of course.

It was only another couple of weeks of all this hoo-ha, and then he would schmooze no more.

He couldn't wait.

'Jake.'

At Ella's soft voice to his left, he rested his glass back on the bar.

"Evening, Ella,' he said as he turned to face her.

He'd planned to say something further, but the words were suddenly clogging his throat.

She looked—and there really was no other word to describe her—spectacular.

She wore a dress of some clingy black fabric that did its job and *clung* all the way from just above her knee to her shoulders. Or, rather, shoulder, as the fabric flowed from just one, leaving the other bare.

Chunky, flat jewels were embroidered densely to the fabric at her collarbone, becoming increasingly more sparse as they travelled towards the upper curve of her breast before blending entirely into black.

Too late, he remembered to look at her face.

When he met her gaze she raised one perfectly arched and bemused eyebrow.

He didn't quite know what to say. Instead, he blindly reached for his beer, and took a long, long drink.

'You look,' he tried, eventually, 'great.'

There was an appalling understatement.

'Thank you,' she said, and her gaze dipped to the floor for a moment. He recognised the action for what it was—a throwback to shy Eleanor, who'd always had difficulty accepting, or believing, compliments. 'I was about to say the same about you.'

She flicked her eyes over the outfit she'd selected for him. 'Nice suit,' she said, wryly.

'I suppose it's not so bad,' he said. This elicited exactly the response he was after—narrowed and flashing angry eyes.

'You're the best-dressed guy here, and you know it.'

He grinned, shrugged as if he couldn't care less and enjoyed Ella's obviously frustrated reaction. She knew perfectly well he was teasing her, and yet she still reacted, despite her best efforts.

In that way, at the very least, Ella hadn't changed at all.

Then she did her little shoulder-straightening thing, and Jake knew he was in for a few minutes of Ella in image-consultant mode.

He didn't mind.

After all, he was the one who'd conspired for her to be here. He hadn't allowed himself to consider in too much detail why he'd done it. If he wanted, he could justify it as a logical business decision. His image consultant 'on tap', so to speak, as he navigated through the treacherous waters of small talk, thick with its heavy infestation of snapping, circling journalist piranhas.

But the real reason had something to do with the woman who'd been prepared to go to battle for him. Who'd laughed uncontrollably with him. Maybe even the woman he'd held in his arms.

He'd missed her.

As he attempted to compute that unexpected possibility, he realised that Ella had been speaking for some time.

'…remember, networking is a lot about listening to what people have to say, rather than… Jake? If you're not listening to me, this is terribly ironic.'

He went to take another long draw of his beer, but it was empty. He busied himself with ordering another drink for the next minute or two. Thinking. Needing not to be looking at her right this instant as he pulled himself together.

'Sorry,' he said, when he turned back to her. 'I'm listening now.'

She'd crossed her arms in front of herself, which had the rather wonderful side effect of emphasising the curves above and below said arms.

'Jake,' she said. Did she guess the direction his thoughts were taking? 'Come on, this is important. You need to focus.'

He nodded, giving all appearances of being suitably contrite. But, in all seriousness, he was having major difficulties concentrating. Ella in that dress did not a work-focused Jake make. He liked her hair loose, too! It was much, much longer than she'd had it as a teenager, and arranged into generous curls that cascaded down her shoulders.

'Okay, so you've got a really diverse crowd here tonight. Journalists—Australian and international, representatives of the chains that will stock the phone, Armada staff members, a few random celebrities, and a varied assortment of the general public.'

'And I need to tailor my message for them all,' he said, and the tension started to ooze back into his body.

'Well, yes and no. The most important thing to remember is to be genuinely excited and enthusiastic about the phone. That type of energy will draw people in.'

He nodded. That part was easy.

'And, as I said,' Ella continued, 'make sure you listen carefully. The journalist from *SmartPhone Monthly* or whatever will want to hear all about the nuts and bolts of the phone. While the starlet from some afternoon soapie wants to learn about the cool stuff she'll actually use. You need to tell her how your phone will make her life easier—*and* make her look ultra fashionable and right on the cutting edge while doing so. You need to frame what you say for your audience.'

Ella then gave a few examples, but this wasn't what Jake was really worried about.

'But what about the non-phone stuff,' he said, 'the small talk and the gossiping?'

That was the bit that he'd been dreading. The fawning and the falseness.

'I wouldn't have picked you as much of a gossip,' Ella said, with a grin, 'but you're not going to have a problem with small talk tonight. I could give you tips to start conversations, like opening with a compliment, but it won't be necessary. You're the star attraction tonight, especially after yesterday.'

Surprisingly—or maybe not, Jake didn't understand all this campaign stuff at all—the Armada marketing department had not been all that upset by Jake's minor radio explosion.

The main gist of it was that it was far from the worst thing that could've happened—an *all publicity is good publicity* kind of situation.

But they'd made it clear, ever so politely, that it would be preferred if it was a one-off.

Jake Donner was to promote the phone and not, by his behaviour, to overshadow the product.

'I'm not so sure about that,' he said. 'So far tonight no one's come to speak to me.'

'That's because your Jake Donner glare would've singed off their eyelashes. I reckon people are thinking I deserve a bravery medal for talking to you now.'

Jake gave a brief, harsh laugh. 'My disdain for the event must have been more obvious than I'd intended.'

'Much more,' she said, 'but that's okay. It's easily fixed. You're looking a lot more approachable now. That little storm cloud of doom seems to have relocated from the space above your head.'

Because of Ella.

'You just need to keep it up. Think friendly and approachable thoughts or something. And remember to smile. You'll be fine. You can be quite charming when you put your mind to it.'

Her gaze dipped again, just for a second or two.

'And if I get any questions I don't want to answer?'

'Easy. If you can't or don't want to, deflect the question, just say "no comment". In a casual environment like this it's not as awkward as when you've got a camera in your face.'

He nodded.

'Okay. So people come up and talk to me. I act all enthusiastic and passionate about the phone.' Ella nodded in encouragement. 'But then what? Once the phone stuff peters out? I've got no intention of pretending to be someone's best friend when I've known them for five minutes. I'm predicting a wave of awkward, long silences.'

'I don't want you to try and be someone you're not. People can smell insincerity, not that I think you're capable of it, anyway. So what I'd suggest, is—'

'Hang on,' Jake cut in. 'Back up a little. Did you really just say that you *don't want me to try and be someone I'm not*?'

'Yes?' Ella replied slowly, her forehead wrinkled in confusion. 'So?'

'Hasn't that been the whole intent of all this?' Jake waved his hand up and down his body. 'For me to become someone I'm not?'

'Absolutely not,' Ella said, with an unexpected bite to her tone. 'My consulting services assist people to present their *best* selves.' Behind her contacts her eyes flashed, and she stepped forward, crowding his personal space. 'Is that what you think I've been doing? Changing you?'

He looked down at himself. At the unfamiliar clothing and shoes. From the corner of his eye he could see the party heaving around him. This was not the native habitat of Jacob Donner.

'Yes.'

Ella closed her eyes for a second, and Jake had the sense she was slowly counting to ten. Then her eyes popped open, and she said, rather calmly: 'Haven't you been paying any attention at all? Everything—your look, the media training, everything I've told you tonight—it's been *all* about you. Not about changing you. Giving you the tools to *be you* in an environment you're uncomfortable in.'

As she watched him, frustration stiffening her body, he figured he'd better give her theory at least a moment's consideration.

Could she be right?

He reconsidered his new wardrobe, his new look. If he was honest, there was not one item of clothing that he vehemently disliked. If he was even more honest, each morning, once he'd got over the strangeness of putting on such different clothes, he'd barely noticed them at all. He'd felt comfortable. Just the same as he did every other day.

Even tonight, in his suit, he felt okay. She'd known he'd never wear a tie. Or shoes with pointy tips. Or skinny-leg trousers. Or put product in his hair.

He was still Jake Donner. Just a little fancier.

And really—*really*—was that such a terrible thing?

Ella must have seen the exact instant that little cog had turned in his brain, as she smiled—a big triumphant smile.

'See?' she said. 'I told you I'm good at my job.' She paused, softening the smugness in her tone just a little. 'Can we get back on track, now, please?'

And then she was off again, with tips and tricks and strategies.

But he wasn't really paying attention, although he was careful she didn't notice.

Because, while he had to concede that Ella was not in the business of making someone pretend to be anything or anyone they weren't, it was impossible to ignore the one significant exception to that rule.

She was standing right in front of him.

Jake had been quite insistent that Ella stay by his side during his first forays into the wonderful world of schmoozing and small talk.

Ostensibly to step in should anything go pear-shaped but Jake was a quick study, and he was doing absolutely fine.

He would never be the life of the party, but who cared? He certainly had the mysterious, handsome and charming thing down pat. He smiled, he subtly promoted the phone, and he nodded and murmured politely when the conversations shot off in all sorts of strange directions. She had no doubt he was bored out of his brain, of course, but he hid it exceedingly well.

So far, her professional advice had been limited to a subtle nudge when he'd started to fidget during a particularly long-winded discussion about the relative merits of two exclusive Sydney fine-dining restaurants, and a whispered *no comment* when he'd started to do his glower thing when questioned about yesterday's radio interview.

With little to do but stand beside him and engage in the conversation of the moment, Ella was finding it increasingly difficult to ignore other things.

Like how she'd felt when he'd first seen her dress and his gaze had as good as caressed her. With just that look, her body had gone white-hot. She'd been so, so aware of him.

It was stupid to be overwhelmed by his appearance. It was hardly a surprise, after all, given that she'd selected everything he wore. And yet here she was, surprised—because she honestly hadn't thought it possible for Jake to become any more handsome. But it had turned out there *was* some room left to ratchet up his sexiness quotient and tonight it was at impossibly impossible levels.

What was it? The glamorous setting, the intimate lighting?

Yes, that must be it.

Although, a perfidious little voice inside her insisted it was none of these things. But instead, it had everything to do with whatever had shifted, or changed, or grown between them when they'd laughed together on that Pyrmont street.

So now, they stood side by side, with *something* that zipped and zinged between them.

The official launch came and went, brief, to the point, and right on 'message'. Jake was doing everything Armada had asked of him, even managing to crack a smile for the bevy of photographers that had appeared like magic as he'd taken to the podium.

Later, once most of the guests had consumed enough alcohol to lose their inhibitions and hit the dance floor, Jake came and stood beside her. She'd stepped out onto the nearly deserted balcony, her champagne glass balanced on a tall cocktail table beside the railing.

'How do you do it?' he asked. 'All this?'

Her lips quirked. 'You mean have a good time?'

'I think you know this isn't my idea of a good time.'

'So what is?' she asked, curious.

'Coding,' he answered, quick as a flash.

Ella smiled fully. Always *such* a geek.

Then he shrugged. 'And, I guess hiking with my dogs up in the mountains. Mountain-bike riding—sometimes with a mate or two. Climbing.'

'Let me guess—in the mountains?'

Now it was his turn to smile. 'It's the best place in the world. I've got my own place up there.'

She knew that, of course. No self-respecting tabloid journalist could let an article go by without some reference to his home. S*ydney's Blue Mountains Billionaire, Software Mogul's Mountain Hideaway* and so on and so forth.

Ella wrinkled her nose. 'I know it's supposed to be beautiful, but I reckon I'd go crazy living that far away from Sydney.'

'I'd go crazy if I lived any closer.' He rested both hands on the balcony railing, and looked out over the harbour. Beneath them, along the edge of the marina, flowed a steady stream of Friday-night revellers, muffled snippets of their conversations mixing with the heavy bass emanating from the party behind them.

'You still haven't answered my question,' he said, after a while. 'I genuinely want to know—how do you stand this?'

'It's really not all that complicated,' she said. 'It's fun. It's the buzz of getting ready. Of meeting new people. Of laughing and chatting and dancing. What isn't there to love?'

He shook his head. 'It's exhausting.'

She shrugged. 'For me it's the opposite. I'd go mad stuck in my apartment all the time. I need noise, and chatter and people. It *gives* me energy.'

'But you must need a break, occasionally?' he asked. He was looking at her as if she were some bizarre software glitch—one that if he stared at long enough would offer up a solution.

'Nope,' she said. 'I like to keep myself busy. Most nights I've got something on—salsa dancing, Pilates, any classes I feel like taking, or just catching up with friends. Cocktails. Dancing, that kind of thing.'

He turned, and leaned back against the railing, studying her.

'But that's new. You used to say you were happiest in your own company. Or, with...'

Me. With Jake.

But of course, he'd left.

Ella laughed, but it sounded about as artificial as it was. 'Ah, the words of a girl not invited to any parties, and with no money to go shopping or to riding lessons.'

'Really?' he said, the word a little hollow. A beat later she realised exactly what he was thinking.

'Oh! I don't mean I didn't like hanging out with you. You were my best friend.' It felt bizarre to say something like that, something so juvenile, to the tall, dark and devastatingly handsome man before her. But it had been true. He'd been her best friend, her only friend. 'But, you know, I also kind of wondered what it would be like to be one of the popular girls.' She held her hands up in a helpless gesture. 'What can I say? I guess it's kind of natural to want what you can't have.'

It was a cliché, a nothing, thoughtless sentence, and yet it was as if they both temporarily stopped breathing.

What they both wanted suddenly made the air between them impossibly thick with delicious, un-ignorable tension.

'What did you want, Ella?'

Oh, that wasn't fair. He knew. She'd told him a very long time ago.

The memory still had the power to make every last remnant of awkward, shy Eleanor want to cringe, then run away and hide.

'What *do* you want, Ella?'

What did she want, right now? Out here, alone with Jake on the balcony, the lights of the Sydney CBD towering and twinkling above them, the beat of the music—or was it something else?—making every cell in her body thrum, and pulse and hum?

'I—'

A high-pitched feminine squeal obliterated the moment before Ella was even absolutely sure what she'd been going to say.

No, that was a lie. She'd known. But she wasn't going to admit to it now.

He was from a past she would *never* revisit. He'd hurt her, once. So much.

She couldn't let that happen again.

Beside them, a woman in a sequined dress staggered to the rail, a man with messy hair and rolled up shirtsleeves holding her up or maybe it was the other way around. 'Great night!' he slurred, with a nod of greeting.

Ella carefully straightened her shoulders. Not that she needed another reason to come to her senses, but Jake was still her client. And she was, technically, working right now.

'Ella?' he said. 'You were saying?'

'Oh,' she said, hoping she sounded as flippant and carefree as she intended as she deliberately rewound to his earlier question. 'Of course I wanted what every unpopular girl wants. A date with the most popular boy at school. Preferably to the school ball.' She managed a smile. 'That's what always happened in all those books I read, or the movies—that scene at the end on the dance floor, so I'd always secretly hoped...'

She was making this up as she went along. Yes, she'd envied the other girls. Yes, she'd wanted the date to the ball.

But it was always Jake who starred in her daydreams.

'Should we go back inside?' she said. 'It's not too late to squeeze in some more schmoozing, I'm sure.'

Jake didn't answer. Instead, he was looking at her in a way that made the hairs at the back of her neck stand on end.

'Jake?'

He reached out, wrapping his much larger hand around hers. His touch shot sensation shivering along her spine, then right down to her French-manicured toes.

He pushed away from the railing, then tugged her along behind him as he headed back inside.

For a few paces she followed, struck somewhat dumb, but then she quite literally dug her heels in, right where the wooden decking of the balcony met the polished boards of the restaurant.

'What are you doing?'

He looked back at her over his shoulder, the lights from inside throwing half his face into shadow.

'I thought we could recreate that scene. On the dance floor.'

Ella shook her head, horror warring with disloyal anticipation. 'Don't be stupid,' her sensible self managed. 'This is no school ball, and you certainly weren't the most popular boy in my year.'

'It's close enough. We've got the dance floor, and there's even a disco ball. Plus—you're the one who called me the star attraction tonight, remember? Tonight I am the popular guy.'

She tried again. 'But why?'

He blinked, as if he hadn't even considered this. Eventually, he spoke. 'Maybe I also wanted things that could never have been.'

His gaze didn't move from hers while he waited for her response.

After what felt like an eternity, she nodded.

And followed him back inside.

CHAPTER TEN

REALITY, ice cold and unyielding, hit about five steps later.

What on earth was she doing?

She needed to stop this. Now.

'Jake?' she said. But her voice was lost in the dull roar of conversation and the near hypnotic beat of the music.

Or maybe Jake was just ignoring her.

She couldn't make a scene. The place was crawling with journalists, desperate for a story about the mysterious and deeply private Jake Donner.

She couldn't do that to him—or to her. The last thing she needed was the media linking her and Jake together. Their shared past was then only a short hop, skip and jump away.

What to do, what to do?

Her brain had deserted her. Years of knowledge used to instruct others how to politely extract themselves from awkward conversations and situations had, to all intents and purposes, completely evaporated.

She had nothing. Her database of gracious refusals was returning no results.

Oh, God, now even her metaphors were tainted by Jake.

Somehow they'd reached the dance floor, Ella's hand still encased in Jake's.

Okay. She had a new plan.

The music was not slow. Not even close. In fact, it bore a far greater resemblance to the soundtrack expected at a Kings Cross nightclub than a slow dance at a Year Twelve Ball.

So she'd just dance for a few minutes with a respectable distance between them. Relocate her ability to form coherent sentences. Then leave.

No problem.

The odds rocketed up highly in favour of her plan succeeding when Jake dropped her hand. No longer could his touch muddle with her synapses.

But then he smiled at her, and that had much the same effect as his touch.

The floor was so packed that dancing wasn't truly a possibility, so they both kind of shuffled to the beat while facing each other. Jake was looking at her, but she made a point of looking anywhere and everywhere except straight back at him.

Pretend you're out with your girlfriends. Relax.

But no matter how hard she tried, or how much effort she applied to focusing on the music, the tension would not flow from her body. And she certainly couldn't switch off her awareness of him.

She tried, so hard, to remember that she was supposed to *like* *t*his. That she'd spent more weekends than she could ever remember out dancing, and that it made her feel good.

If she'd danced with quite possibly thousands of strangers over the years, why not dance with Jake? Same difference, right?

And, slowly, eventually and remarkably something changed.

She realised her smile wasn't forced. She could feel the beat as it reverberated through her body. Her movements became loose and easy and as natural as breathing.

It was all about the music, and dancing and fun.

And she forgot that she shouldn't be looking at Jake.

At first her gaze was sensibly trained at a button on his shirt, but it wasn't long before the crowded floor became even more crowded, and she was pushed close enough to him that she was forced to look up.

Her redirected attention again started somewhere safe: the skin exposed by the two buttons she'd recommended he leave undone.

It was nice, innocent skin at the base of his neck.

Unfortunately, she knew exactly how he'd look if he unbuttoned another button. Or five. Or all of them.

She'd done so well with limiting how often she'd allowed herself to remember exactly how amazing Jake had looked without his shirt that day in the change room. To, oh, no more than several dozen times.

At seventeen he'd had a very nice chest, she'd thought. At thirty, it had broadened, and gained all sorts of lovely muscles and dips courtesy of all his mountain-related activities, she assumed. And it felt gorgeous, too, firm and solid and strong. But she'd only felt it against her cheek when he'd held her. How would it feel beneath her fingers?

With an effort, she halted that traitorous train of thought. She needed to look somewhere else. Immediately.

So she did. This time she chose his chin. It was a nice chin, with sharp, well-defined lines. Pleasingly cleft-free, too. And was that just the slightest hint of a five o'clock shadow?

Yes. She believed it was.

Unfortunately chins were not particularly interesting, and all too soon her gaze crept up, just a little bit further.

To his mouth.

Now she *knew* this wasn't a good place to look, but she found herself quite compelled to do so. And besides, Ella told herself, it was just a *mouth.* Everyone had one. As long as it stayed well away from her, it wasn't doing anyone any harm.

So she took her time exploring its shape as they danced—trying to study him objectively, as if his mouth belonged to no one in particular, and certainly not to Jake.

As she did so she noticed other facts in her periphery. The most surprising being that Jake wasn't that bad a dancer.

He wouldn't go as far as to say he was *good,* but for a bona fide computer geek, he was hardly embarrassing himself. Far, far from it.

So that was one thing she noticed as she focused on his mouth.

Another thing she noticed, this one not so much surprising, but more troubling, was that there was a lot of touching happening around them. The music had mellowed, and with it the mass of dancers had naturally metamorphosed into a collection of twosomes.

Just out of the corner of her left eye, Ella could see a man's strong hand on the small of a woman's back. So chaste, and yet—so not at all. Then, to her right, a woman's hand curled behind a man's neck, her red-tipped fingers lightly caressing his skin, then reaching up to tangle in his hair as she pulled him down for a…

Jake really did have an amazing mouth. Without an ounce of femininity he managed to have lips that looked firm and strong but still utterly kissable. And when he smiled, when those lips kicked up into something sexy and cheeky and smart, well. Quite simply he was near impossible to resist.

Too late she realised he *was* smiling. Smiling at her. And she had at some point inexplicably moved closer. Or maybe he'd moved closer to her. Either way, they were no longer dancing, and instead were kind of swaying on the spot, side to side, and maybe towards each other…

What do you want, Ella?

No. She couldn't allow herself to want this.

She needed to take a step backwards, literally and figuratively, and it was hard—so hard—to make herself do so.

But she managed, at least the physical bit, and when the action bumped her into another dancer the subsequent jumble of apologies did an excellent job of diluting the tension.

Or at least she thought it did.

She made it off the dance floor, for once uncaring what anyone thought. Right now she just needed to be gone. Away.

But when she made it past the bar, through the front door of the restaurant and into the softly lit empty staircase that would lead her outside, Ella didn't feel calm at all.

The reason for this became obvious when she heard a deep voice behind her.

'I guess you're going, then?'

She didn't bother to slow down or look over her shoulder. 'Uh-huh.'

What else could she do? What had been about to happen on the dance floor?

She didn't want to think about it.

With a hand on the railing, she skipped down the stairs as quickly as possible. The theme of the restaurant was followed throughout the entire building, with even these lowly stairs as lush and rich as the restaurant itself, with deep plum carpets and damask wallpaper in shades of gold. Not that she felt much like admiring her surroundings at the moment. At this moment, she just wanted to get out, into a cab, and go home. Right now.

'Ella,' Jake said, much more forcefully this time, strong enough for her to pause at the landing and turn to face him.

'What?' she asked as he came to a stop before her.

But he didn't stop. Instead, he came closer, as close as they'd been on the dance floor.

And then, when her shoulders bumped against the wallpaper, even closer again. Close enough that his height and width seemed to surround her, overwhelm her.

His closeness made her traitorous body react in all the wrong ways: her belly flooded with warmth, her breath hitched, her hands itched to reach and touch him—anywhere—and bring him even closer.

No. That was crazy. This was crazy.

She didn't want any of this. After today she was meant to never see Jake again.

And she'd been glad. Relieved about that. *Hadn't she?*

But feeling this, wanting this, was not good at all.

'Jake…' she started, but the touch of his hand on her cheek silenced her. His fingers slid down slowly, the lightest touch at her temple, her cheek, her jaw, and then, finally, beneath her chin, tilting her mouth upwards. Up towards his.

She swallowed, trying desperately to capture just one lucid, sensible sentence from within a brain that suddenly felt as light and fluffy and insubstantial as fairy floss.

But she found nothing. Maybe she didn't really want to.

'I'll tell you what I wanted,' he said, his voice like velvet. 'And what I want.'

Ella finally let her gaze rise up to meet his—intense, and intimate and hotter than anything she'd ever experienced.

'This,' he said.

Now she expected him to kiss her. Something hard and fast and full of thirteen years of missed opportunities, mistakes and regret.

But that wasn't what she received. Instead he lowered his head ever so slowly.

She had the strangest sense that she was about to fall into the heat she saw in his eyes, into the sensations that zipped about her body, and perhaps even into somewhere further. Somewhere deep inside her that for far too long she'd ignored.

And while it was scary and confusing and complicated, the absolute last thing it felt was *wrong*.

So when his lips finally touched hers, she let herself go.

This was not the kiss of a fumbling, unsure teenager. Oh, no. This Jake was all grown up.

His lips were firm and sure, but not demanding—yet.

He teased her with kisses that were brief, almost chaste, teasing her until she leant into him, until her hands crept up to his shoulders, one remaining to trace the shape and strength of his back, and the other travelling up and into his hair.

But not for a moment did Ella think he was giving her control. This was his kiss; of that she had no doubt. He was, however, giving her time.

Which was all very nice of him, but completely unnecessary.

Her fingers tightened as she tugged him closer, just as his tongue brushed her bottom lip. She shuddered at that unbelievable sensation, and the next thing she knew their kisses were open, voracious and delicious. Their tongues tangled as their sighs, even their breathing, became near indistinguishable as his or hers.

Then he finally touched her, with hands that made her skin burn and the thin fabric of her dress seem an impossibly unfair barrier to the kind of closeness she suddenly desperately wanted.

Skin to skin.

As his fingers traced the curve of her hips, the dip of her waist, and then, ever so slowly, crept higher—but nowhere near high enough—that want became a need.

'Ella,' he said, so close she felt as well as heard him speak. That was all he said, but she knew exactly what he meant.

This was crazy.

She kissed him again, telling him with lips and tongue and teeth how good this felt, how every touch of his hands, every touch of his mouth triggered a rush of sensation that was like nothing else she'd ever experienced.

This was insane.

But then, one moment she was all but wrapped around him, the next he was stepping away, turning his back.

Ella swallowed a whimper. *A whimper?*

Since when did Ella Cartwright *whimper?*

As she processed that unexpected, and previously undiscovered, reaction, her surroundings slowly came back into focus.

They were standing in the landing of a staircase. A public staircase.

'I thought I heard someone,' Jake said.

Oh, God.

Ella focused firmly on the straps of her stilettos and, belatedly, she blushed fiercely.

She hugged herself, keeping her eyes trained determinedly downwards.

How had she just let this happen?

'Hey, don't stress. No one's here. I must have imagined it,' Jake said.

Ella sank back against the wall in relief.

What if someone from the media had seen them?

Jake had turned back to face her, still so, so close.

Incredibly her gaze wanted *so badly* to drift downwards to his mouth. But that was not going to happen again. It couldn't.

'Ella, I—'

'Wow, I'm exhausted,' she said, telling herself she had no interest in hearing whatever Jake was about to say.

Ella managed a serviceable fake yawn. 'I'm going to go find a taxi.'

She didn't give him a chance to reply, and instead just stepped neatly past him.

As fast as she could, she hurried down the steps, the thud of her heels on the thick carpet almost matching the rapid thud of her heart.

That kiss had been too much. Too good, too perfect, too *right*.

She couldn't do this with Jake. She just couldn't.

What if she fell for him again?

Oh, who was she kidding? She had a horrible feeling that it wasn't even a 'what if' in this equation. It was a 'when'.

Outside, the cool air was like a slap to her face. She took a deep breath and arranged her features into something bland and neutral. Up the street she saw the lights of a taxi, and she stuck out a hand to flag it down.

Jake appeared beside her, but she offered him barely a glance. When the taxi pulled to a stop, she yanked open the door, and, with it as a barrier between them, finally forced herself to look at him.

He did not look impressed.

'Ella, what is this? Why are you running away?'

She bristled. 'What, Jake? You don't like it when it's someone else doing the running?'

He went absolutely still.

She continued in clipped and cold syllables. 'That was a kiss that was thirteen years too late, don't you think?'

'Ella, I—'

'Goodbye, Jake,' she said, sliding onto the taxi's vinyl seat.

And with that she closed the door, probably with far more force than was necessary.

Jake immediately rested his hands on the roof of the car, leaning forward so his face and shoulders filled the window.

'Ella, *stop*.'

'Is he with you?' the driver asked over his shoulder.

But Ella kept her eyes trained steadfastly forward, pretending she couldn't see Jake just inches away through the glass.

'No,' she said, her throat suddenly tight. 'Not at all.'

CHAPTER ELEVEN

THE next day Jake knocked—politely—on Ella's door. Just a couple of sharp raps of his knuckles on the solid wooden surface. Very civilised for eight on a Saturday morning.

Then he waited.

When no sound was forthcoming, besides the muffled sound of music playing, he tried again. A bit longer this time. The raps a little more—*clear.*

When this was also unsuccessful, he went with a steady, slow, ponderous knock that he was pretty sure would irritate a bear out of hibernation.

With this, he had success.

The scrape and click of a door unlocking and a chain being unhooked was preceded by soft thuds and thumps and a croaky sounding: *'Who is it?'*

He didn't bother to answer. When she finally pulled open the door, he meant to give her a lecture about opening her door to strangers, but the words got all jammed up in his throat.

She stood in the doorway, one hand still propped against the open door, in a pale pink singlet and purple polka dotted boxer shorts. And that was it.

He wasn't exactly sure what he *expected* her to be wearing, but it wasn't this. It wasn't shorts that revealed miles of bare golden skin and a threadbare singlet that left *very* little to the imagination.

With her hair scraped off her face in a loose, looped-up ponytail and her face make-up free, she *was* beautiful.

How could he have ever, ever thought she was anything else?

He swallowed, and tried to remember where he'd left his ability to speak.

Ella pushed the door fully open and crossed her arms in front of herself. And then, as if only just realising what her top revealed, she slid her arms just a little bit higher, to hide the curves of her breasts. A blush pinkened her cheeks.

'What the hell are you doing here?' she demanded, anger obvious in every tense line of her body. 'How do you know where I live? And—hang on—how did you even get in? This is a secure building.'

He shrugged. 'You're listed in the phone book—it wasn't hard. And you may want to have a word to your neighbour. She recognised me from that article in the *Herald* this week, and when I said I knew you she was happy to let me in.'

'Humpphh,' she muttered indistinctly, then reached for the door, obviously about to slam it in his face. This slamming-of-doors-in-his-face thing was rapidly getting old.

As he wasn't the type of guy to shove his way into a woman's house he figured he'd better start talking. Quickly.

'I haven't answered your question,' he said, 'about why I'm here.'

She paused mid swing. 'Fine,' she said. 'So tell me.'

She gave a little yawn, as if he were the most terribly boring thing she'd ever seen. But was that the slightest flicker of interest in her gaze?

She could lie to herself all she wanted, but he wasn't about to.

He hadn't been able to stop thinking about her last night. About that kiss.

That mad, intense, unexpected kiss.

And also, about what she'd said. *You don't like it when it's someone else doing the running.*

'Something's been bothering me,' he said.

Ella raised her eyebrows. He could pretty much read her mind: *What's bothering me right now is that you're standing on my doorstep at eight on a Saturday morning.*

'You've lived in Sydney for, what, nine years?'

'Eight,' she corrected, looking an adorable mix of sleepy, angry and confused.

'And you've never been up to the mountains.'

She sighed, and reached again for the door. 'Trust me, I don't stay up at night distressed by that gaping hole in my life. Now, if you'll excuse me, I—'

'Oh, come on, Ella. That's a bit hypocritical, isn't it?'

Her arm stilled. 'Pardon me?'

'I haven't been harbouring a desperate need for a makeover, but I gave that a go.'

Her eyes narrowed. 'And you were *such* a conscientious pupil.'

Jake grinned. 'Not at first, I'll admit. But you were right, last night. This whole image rebranding thing, it's been good for me.'

He had the pleasure of watching Ella's jaw drop.

'So I'd like to do something for you. Take you up to the mountains.'

'I've heard about your place. I get that it's beautiful, and peaceful, but it's not my thing.' Then she paused. 'And more to the point, I was *paid* to be your image consultant. There is no favour to be returned.'

For the first time since he'd arrived, he registered the music playing inside Ella's apartment.

'You were asleep when I got here, right?' he asked.

She nodded, looking a little thrown by the change of subject. 'Yes. Why?'

'Then why is there music on?'

'Oh, I don't like silence,' she said, very matter of fact, and then added another nonchalant little yawn. 'Are we done? I'd like to go back to bed.'

The pairing of the concepts of *bed* and *Ella* scrambled his thoughts momentarily, and he wasn't sure he'd heard her correctly.

'You don't like silence?'

The concept floored him. He personally couldn't get enough of the stuff.

'Not particularly,' she said, reaching again for the door. 'Okay? Can you go now?'

'No,' he said. Firmly.

This seemed to surprise Ella. 'Pardon me?'

'Haven't you heard that old adage? Turnabout is fair play?'

She watched him steadily for a few minutes, as if weighing something up. 'It's an idiom,' she said, eventually.

'A what?'

'What you just said.' She sighed. 'It's an idiom. And it's supposed to be about shared suffering. You just told me you like your new image.'

Ella always was better than him at English.

'But I *have* suffered,' he said with a grin. 'The launch party last night, the interviews so far and the many more to come.'

But the fact was, with Ella's help, he was dreading them marginally less.

'Then take Armada's board of executives up to your mountain,' she said. 'The campaign and your interview schedule had nothing to do with me.'

Knowing he was mere seconds away from a door slamming that now seemed inevitable, Jake decided to ignore all previous platitudes about not shoving himself into a woman's apartment. He stepped forward, just far enough so that closing the door was now impossible.

Ella's eyes blazed. 'Hey! That's not cool. I—'

'Ella,' he said, leaning forward and catching her gaze with his. 'I want to spend the day with you.'

Jake knew this subtle echo from last night was a risk—but the thing was, it was as simple, and as complicated, as that.

What do you want, Ella?

The unspoken question hung between them.

'Jake, I—'

'That's all I want, Ella. Just today.'

If he thought beyond that, it all became too messy and complicated.

'What would be the point?' she asked, sounding as defeated as she had last night.

'Does there even have to be one? All I want to do is show you something, and I'm trying not to overthink why.'

But he did know the reason. Thirteen years ago she thought he'd run away from her. He couldn't end it this time with Ella running away from him.

This felt...*unfinished.*

He went to run a hand through his hair, before realising it was now far too short for the gesture.

Ella wasn't convinced. She was chewing on her lip and every line of tension in her body was pre-empting a definite *no.*

'Please,' he said, then swallowed. Why were these words suddenly so hard to say? 'Come with me to the mountains. Let me show you something special.'

Her expression shifted. Her eyes widened as she digested what he'd said.

'You don't invite anyone up to your place,' she said, as if she'd just remembered that.

'Exactly,' he said.

It should've been a difficult decision, but it had been anything but.

He'd woken up that morning knowing exactly what he had to do. Beyond today, he had no idea. But right this moment he wanted to share the mountains with Ella.

It took a really long time, but finally she nodded.

'Fine,' she said, sounding about as excited as he'd felt when she'd taken him shopping. She began to close the door. 'Give me a few minutes to get dressed.'

'Make sure you wear comfortable shoes,' he said, relishing the chance to direct Ella's clothing choices.

He could hear her groan well after the door had slammed shut.

Ella had expected the long drive up to Blackheath, the small Blue Mountains town where Jake lived, to be painfully awkward. She'd imagined long, tension-filled silences. Polite, stilted conversations that led nowhere. And the memory of the night before to hover unspoken between them—shared memories of a kiss that had been as delicious as it had been unwise. And of a friendship that had ended so abruptly.

She'd only been partially right. Yes, the electricity of their kiss had not abated, and its presence underlined every word they spoke. But the awkwardness—it was not there at all.

They fell into easy conversation, a familiar rhythm despite the long years they'd been out of practice.

They spoke of nothing in particular, really. They both carefully avoided anything too taboo. Obviously the previous night being the very, very top of that list.

But they also avoided anything to do with work—with Armada, with her business, and definitely anything related to the campaign. It was as if, through mutual agreement, they'd decided to quarantine this day from anything too serious. Anything too complicated.

That suited her just fine.

Just like that day after the radio interview, she was reminded why, so long ago, they'd been near inseparable. It hadn't just been because they were both outsiders at their exclusive high school, although ostracism had certainly pushed them closer.

Ostracism would kind of do that.

On the surface, they hadn't had much in common. But they'd effortlessly spent hours together—talking or not, just hanging out. Laughing at each other's bad jokes, that sort of thing.

It was weird how she'd forgotten all that.

At first, a small, persistent voice in her head kept telling her—in no uncertain terms—that this was *not* a good idea. It nagged and nagged and nagged.

But then, she'd stopped making decisions based on whether her actions were good ideas or not about half an hour ago, when she'd agreed to come with him.

Actually, her questionable decision-making had started well before then. In fact, every decision she'd made in the past twelve or so hours—save walking away from Jake after their kiss—had been a very, very long way from sensible.

So, overall, it seemed a bit late to behave any differently.

She decided Jake was right. This was just for today.

And so she silenced those pesky voices of reason.

And it felt good.

What didn't feel so good, however, was hiking a million miles up a mountain.

It *was* beautiful out here. She couldn't argue with that.

Beautiful and steep. Her aching legs told her so with every, single, seemingly never-ending step.

They'd walked for ages along the Megalong Valley, amongst blue gums that towered so high they as good as touched the sky. They were, unbelievably, still on Jake's property, and his Pointers—who must be the luckiest dogs in the world to have all this space as their backyard—galumphed and leapt in ecstatic loops around them. And behind them. And ahead of them.

Their joy for life was contagious.

It was a glorious winter's day, and with the sun shining and a guide who looked rather hot in his cargo shorts, Ella could think of a lot worse ways to spend her Saturday. Even if this wasn't the Saturday she'd intended.

While the terrain had been relatively flat, Ella had been feeling quietly smug. It would seem that all of her dancing, plus her weekly Pilates classes, were the perfect training ground for the weekend mountain hiker.

Or so she'd thought.

As they'd begun their climb to the rather unoriginally titled 'Look Out' her erroneous smugness would've been comical if she'd been in any shape to laugh.

Jake, who wasn't even close to breaking a sweat, despite also carrying a backpack containing their lunch, would occasionally pause up ahead on the track and wait patiently for her.

At this point he would also offer 'helpful' suggestions regarding her technique, which, as it was to *get up this damn mountain in any way possible*, led to some less than gracious reactions. The primary one being a narrow-eyed glare.

Frustratingly, this just seemed to make his grin broader.

As they walked further from the valley floor, the trees grew sparse and the shrubby understory thicker and more colourful. Some of the plants she recognised, like the banksias with their spikes of tightly packed yellow flowers, while others were unfamiliar, and she'd call out to Jake to identify them. Jake, of course, knew them all.

But finally the narrow little track opened up to an almost bald clearing of pale sandstone and tufts of dark green grasses.

At first, she was so thrilled to have reached their destination that all she was capable of was closing her eyes and letting the slightest of breezes cool her skin. Only when her breathing slowed down to close to normal did she look at the view.

And what a view it was.

Above the irregular patchwork of cleared farmland and dense forest that covered the valley floor, sheer sandstone cliffs rose high and proud, harsh and abrupt with their sharp-edged rectangular angles. But beyond the drama of the cliffs were hills and peaks as far as the eye could see, undulating haphazardly beneath the haze of blue that gave the mountains their name.

'Pretty special, isn't it?' Jake asked, walking up to where she stood, well back from the edge of the cliff. 'And this is nothing like the proper lookouts like Govett's Leap or Pulpit Rock, but then, I can't take the dogs onto the national park and I don't like leaving them behind. You should go check those out some time, too.'

At her look of horror he smiled. 'Don't panic, you can drive up pretty close to those ones. Only a short walk to the view.'

She noticed he didn't offer to take her, and she had the oddest sense of disappointment.

Why? This was a one-off.

There was absolutely no reason for him to take her hiking ever again. There was also absolutely no reason for her to *want* to go hiking again. Quite apart from her current state of exhaustion and—probably temporary—hatred for all things hiking, until about three hours ago she'd believed that Jake Donner was, once again, out of her life.

It had even been *her* decision.

She needed to remember that.

While she'd been enjoying the view, Jake had tied the dogs to a tree, and when she looked over her shoulder she could see their bodies stretched out long, their eyes closed as they recovered from their mountain-climbing adventure.

As beautiful as the view was, she envied them. A nap sounded *very* tempting.

Reading her thoughts, Jake jerked his head to where he'd dumped his backpack. 'Come on, let's have some lunch. You look like you need some sustenance.'

This was very true.

A few minutes later they sat cross-legged on a quilted blanket, their picnic lunch of very exotic ham and cheese sandwiches spread out before them.

Oh, and he'd also brought a bottle of champagne.

It was perfect.

Again, slowly but surely, they began to talk, immediately breaking their unspoken agreement to keep their conversation uncomplicated. Ella was surprised to realise she didn't mind.

'What happened,' Jake said quietly, 'after I left?'

The question didn't sound at all random.

Ella sipped her champagne, looking out at the view and not at Jake.

'You mean at school?'

'Yeah. And everywhere else, I guess. It must've been so hard for you, and for your dad.'

The bubbly liquid in her throat was suddenly more difficult to swallow.

'Well,' she said, trying to sound light, as if none of it mattered. 'Unsurprisingly, school pretty much sucked. No instant popularity. No sympathy vote to get me into the cool crowd.'

That poor effort at black humour made Jake's gaze soften.

'Were you okay?'

Without me?

That was what he was really asking. 'Of course I was,' she said, firmly.

And she was. Okay. Not good, certainly, not as good as when she'd had her parents and Jake. Not even close to good really. For years.

But she'd survived.

Jake looked sceptical. Worried. But he didn't push.

'When I heard about your dad…' he started. A pause. 'It just wasn't fair. He was a good man.'

She smiled. 'An eccentric man,' she said, remembering his crazy beard, obsession with incense and insatiable appetite for long, knowledgeable discussions about the environment and government policy. She'd loved him. 'It was a long time ago now, nine years, almost. It was a blessing, in a way, as he was never the same without my mum.'

'He was lucky to have you.'

'Maybe,' she replied with a shrug, but the simple gesture was really wildly inappropriate.

Jake's forehead wrinkled. 'What does that mean?'

'Do you remember how he pretty much shut up shop when my mum died? He barely said a word. Didn't seem to listen all that much, either.'

He nodded.

'Well, he never got any better.'

That didn't even begin to describe the reality of what had happened to her father. But then, how did you put into words or actions the reality of dealing with a man who once adored you, but was suddenly utterly remote?

It was impossible.

'I had no idea,' Jake said, his voice heavy with regret. He shifted on the blanket, fidgeting as he rearranged his frame. 'I told myself you'd be okay, that you had your dad who loved you, and that you didn't need me.'

'I didn't *need* you,' she said, and as she spoke she realised it was true. 'Sure, I missed you. Heaps. And it hurt, for a really, really long time.'

Ella somehow knew that now was not the time to sugar-coat.

'Ella—'

She cut him off.

'It was good, in a way, you know?'

He watched her blankly.

'I mean to get over it. To get over needing people.' She shrugged. 'It taught me an important lesson. I need to rely on just me. No one else.'

That way no one could let her down. No one she needed could leave her.

'That's not right, Ella. Of course you need people.'

She laughed. 'Seriously, Jake? You're telling *me* I need people? Who, exactly, do you need, Jake?'

Who have you ever needed?

He went silent.

'You're different,' Jake said, after a while. 'You were brought up surrounded by love. Giving love. You do need people. You do need love.'

She shook her head. Maybe once, but not any more.

Now she had a life full of fun and laughter and activity. No pain. No loss.

'But that doesn't apply to you?' she asked.

He leant back onto his elbows on the blanket. 'I'm not like you,' he said, as if that explained everything.

'Do you mean because of your parents?'

He sucked in a sharp breath. She knew, without a smidgen of doubt, that she was the only person Jake would ever let ask him this question.

Rather than making her feel good, she felt sad. So sad for him.

'Did I tell you how my dad told me he loved me every single day? Every single day he told me I was his favourite boy. The best son in the world. That he'd love me for ever.'

No. He'd never spoken about his father.

She didn't bother replying and, besides, Jake wasn't waiting for her answer.

'And you know all about my mum. And her emotions, the highs, the lows. The *love*.'

He all but spat the word out, like a curse.

He'd been looking out at nothing, over the edge of the cliff, but now he turned to her, meeting her eyes. 'Is it all that surprising that I don't know what to do with….' a long, long pause '…emotions.'

That hadn't been what he was going to say.

'And I certainly don't know what to do with other people's,' he said.

He was explaining, Ella realised. Why he'd never emailed, or called, or sent her that postcard.

'You didn't know what to do with me,' she said, with a sad smile.

He nodded. 'Or with my mum. She was just so *much*, so much emotion, so many highs and lows.' Jake swallowed. 'I don't feel like that, you know? I don't have those feelings. I don't get love. Not then, and not now.'

Ella remembered the magazine articles, his heartbroken ex-girlfriend and the headlines: *Georgina McAvoy's exclusive claims—Jake Donner—what you see is all you get.*

Had she run away from Jake last night for exactly the same reasons? Couldn't she handle the way he made her feel?

Well, yes.

But with Jake, it was more than that. She'd had to teach herself to keep her distance, to hold her emotions in check. With Jake it was who he was.

Ella couldn't kid herself, if she let herself, she was capable of love.

And with Jake, that could only end one way.

She would not put herself through that again.

'You were right, you know, last night,' Jake said. 'That kiss was thirteen years too late.'

'No,' she said, 'I was wrong. Kissing me then, or kissing me now—the outcome is the same.' She went quiet for a long moment. 'Isn't it?'

She *hated* the hope in those words.

His gaze met hers again. He didn't say a word, but they both knew the answer.

The answering ache was now so familiar that she barely registered it.

As if she wanted more, anyway. As if she wanted love.

She'd come to Sydney determined to fill her life with fun, and glitz, and glamour, to create a world without a hint of the loss and the rejection of her past. Her friendships, both male and female, never, ever scratched beneath the surface.

Although she wasn't like Jake. She believed in love.

It just wasn't for her.

Neither of them spoke for the longest time.

Ella's gaze drifted to the view, and the seemingly endless mountains that stretched all the way to the horizon. Eventually the atmosphere shifted—as if all this space had diluted their pain. Their regret.

Slowly, infinitesimally, the silence gained a different hue. A lightness.

'How's the silence going for you?' Jake asked, and his tone was completely different from before. He even managed a smile as he looked at her. 'Driving you crazy, yet?'

'You know, it hasn't,' she said, surprised.

'Make sure you pay attention to it. To the silence. It helps.'

She raised an eyebrow. 'That sounds like something my hippy parents would have said.'

'Just trust me,' he said. 'Lay back, shut your eyes, and listen to it.'

It was on the tip of her tongue to point out that little contradiction, but she did as he asked, stretching herself out on the blanket, her legs crossed at her ankles and her hands resting lightly on her tummy, just above the waistband of her jeans.

It wasn't that big a blanket, and so when she shut her eyes it took her a *long* time to concentrate on anything but the man lying beside her. Despite everything they'd just said—it was impossible for her to forget, or to dismiss, their kiss.

How simple it would be to turn onto her side and reach for him, to pull him towards her and feel the delicious weight of him.

Her whole body thrummed with the compulsion to do exactly that, even if it was only for today.

But she was determined—absolutely determined—to ignore it.

She'd made the right decision last night. The only possible one. Their conversation had only confirmed in a million different ways how right she'd been.

So she was going to lie here and *only* listen to the silence. Even if it killed her.

Finally—surprisingly—her thoughts did drift away from Jake.

Ever so slowly she began to realise that the silence wasn't silent at all. Around them the mountains overflowed with noise, she just had to be perfectly quiet to hear it.

Little puffs of wind rustled the leaves of the eucalypts. Somewhere nearby she heard the muted song of a magpie, and a few minutes later the laughing call of a kookaburra.

Closer to where they lay the shrubs and trees that surrounded them would creak and sigh as something moved amongst them. Jake had said that kangaroos, echidnas and wombats lived up here so Ella decided to attribute the sounds to one or more of those animals, and *not* to the snakes and lizards he'd also described.

Gradually she let her body relax, and her mind empty to anything but the mountains.

It was lovely. Seriously lovely. An escape from reality. *Their* reality.

For about five minutes.

'Uh, Jake?' she said, perfectly aware she was probably breaking some sacred mountain silence code, but unable to lie still another second longer. 'This is all very nice and everything, but...'

A laugh was her reply. A belly-deep, chest-rumbling laugh.

Ella's eyes popped open and she rolled onto her side to face him. He'd already done the same, and he watched her with laughter in his palest blue eyes, his body still shaking with mirth.

'But what, Ella?' he said.

She tried to keep a straight face, not completely comfortable at being the subject of such hilarity. 'Well,' she said, stiffly because otherwise she'd smile, 'it does get kind of boring after a while.' Now her mouth curved upwards despite her best efforts. 'Come on, you've got to admit that.'

He just shook his head where it rested on the arm he'd hooked beneath his neck, his bicep an impressive pillow of sorts. And he still smiled the broadest of smiles.

'Two minutes, Ella.'

She sniffed, although her attempts at affronted displeasure fell largely flat. 'It was at least five,' she said haughtily.

This started his laughter all over again, and before she knew it she was laughing too, laughing because she had the attention span of a gnat, laughing because the dogs started barking, laughing because she'd just walked up the side of a mountain, and laughing because she was lying in the sun next to Jake. And he was laughing with her.

It took ages, but eventually their laughter morphed from wildly raucous to that hiccupping type where just as you thought you were done a little burst of laughter would break free, as if not quite ready for the world to be serious again.

As they had that day in the street. And as they had probably a hundred times before.

But, then, even that ended. And they were just two people, looking at each other—grinning at each other—across a blanket. Alone.

Ella looked down at where her right hand lay, curled and relaxed on the blanket. Not even a foot away was Jake's hand. Big, dark and strong-looking beside her long, skinny fingers and their manicured nails.

She hadn't noticed before, but the pattern of the blanket created a solid red line between them, the bright fabric the vertical stroke of a cross that intersected the quilt and provided a border to the complicated multicoloured smaller squares.

The line was almost exactly in the middle.

At the moment, Ella was entirely on her side. Jake was entirely on his.

They'd both gone silent, and once again the only sound was that of the surrounding bushland.

Even the dogs had settled. She heard one of them sigh behind her as he or she reorganised themselves beneath their tree.

Ella knew it was only a matter of time before she or Jake shifted. Before one of their hands crept forward, tentatively, to touch the other's.

She knew it, as well as she knew the earth was round, that she never kept her new year's resolutions and that she looked absolutely dreadful in high-waisted trousers.

It was inevitable. This day was inevitable.

'Ella...' he murmured, and it was a whisper, and a groan and a promise all wrapped into one.

Yet, she'd been wrong. He didn't grab her hand, or even touch it. Instead, in a movement she barely registered, he was above her, his elbows holding his weight, his big hands on either side of her face, cradling her gently. For his kiss.

His lips touched hers with intent. No waiting this time. No politeness, no caution, and definitely not a hint of surprise.

Had there ever been anything more certain than this kiss?

Ella lost herself to the incredible sensation of his mouth on hers, letting her body go languid as electricity sparked wherever there bodies touched. Her hands went wild as they roamed over his back, voraciously exploring its muscled topography, the furrow of his spine and then dipping under the hem of his T-shirt to feel warm, smooth, tempting skin.

His mouth tasted just slightly of champagne, but the dance of his tongue was as seductive and mind-altering as the strongest, most potent of alcohols.

When his lips left hers she gasped in disappointment, only to sigh when he trailed kisses along her jaw, and then again when he finally, finally, sunk his body partially onto hers.

Oh, that felt good.

Then his hands were on her, in all the right places, and their legs were intertwined, and her body was telling her in every way possible how absolutely right this all was.

Then their eyes met, and Jake smiled at her.

'Your eyes are brown today,' he said, and for the first time Ella realised she'd forgotten all about her emerald-green contacts in the crazy unexpectedness of that morning.

So she looked up at Jake, with her plain old eyes, and while she didn't fully understand why, she realised she was glad.

Then her lashes fluttered shut, and she lost herself to the moment, and to Jake, and to the majesty of the mountains.

CHAPTER TWELVE

ELLA woke amongst a tangle of bed sheets, the bright and unforgiving mid-morning light making her blink, and blink again.

Still on her back, she stretched, her arms reaching upwards so her fingers brushed against the jarrah bed head, while her toes curled into the loveliness of bazillion-thread-count cotton.

Mmmmmmm.

She turned her head, on the mattress and not on her pillow as it had been long ago lost to the floor, to face Jake. He'd pushed himself up on an elbow, his chin propped against his palm. Actually, he looked pretty much identical to how he'd looked on that blanket up at the lookout.

Except, of course, for the whole totally naked thing.

She smiled.

Mmmmmmmm.

Ella knew that, right about now, she should be well on her way to a great big flurry of spectacular panic. It was Sunday morning. Their day was over.

What had she done? What was she doing?

But up here in Jake's bedroom, the curtainless windows showcasing the valley and *exactly* how totally alone they both were, she honestly didn't want to think about it.

Right now she was more than happy to cover her ears to all that was sane and sensible, and instead simply bask in the appreciation of Jake's gaze and the memories of the past twenty-four hours.

On second thoughts, no…basking would be a terrific waste of time.

Instead, she reached for Jake, he reached for her, and for the next long while Ella happily stopped worrying about thinking about anything at all.

He should be hating this.

Jake considered this as he sat, quite comfortably, in this little scene of domesticity. Ella had dozed off not long after the opening credits, and in her sleep had gradually moved closer until she now had her head nestled against his shoulder, and his arm was wrapped around hers.

Given the way they'd spent the past day, it had been kind of ridiculous how they'd both just stared at his couch in confusion once they'd made the decision to leave his bedroom and watch a movie. Should they sit close, all couple-like? Or more as they had in high school, each unselfconsciously doing whatever felt comfortable? This had generally involved Jake sprawled with his legs stretched out long, and Ella with her legs curled up under herself neatly. And masses of space between them—increasingly more with each passing year as they'd both started to feel—and ignore—that pull of teenage attraction.

In the end, this afternoon, by unspoken agreement, they'd compromised.

They'd sat, not touching, but close enough that doing so would be so, so easy.

And then, when Ella had fallen asleep, they'd ended up all wrapped around each other anyway.

He didn't hate this, not at all. In fact, it was kind of nice.

Ella had left her hair loose, and so it spread haphazardly over her shoulders and onto him in messy waves. She did, however, wear make-up. Her bottomless handbag had produced an emergency stash of blush and mascara—or whatever it was she put on her face. So even in sleep, she was perfectly presented. His insistence that she didn't need make-up, especially up here, had been met with a laugh and total disbelief.

Watching her as she slept, he was disappointed. He remembered when her eyelashes had been almost translucent, and when he'd been able to count the freckles on her nose.

At least, a little earlier, he'd managed to divest her of her glasslike lip-gloss in the most enjoyable way possible.

A few days ago he could never have imagined this weekend they'd just spent together: walking, drinking wine, laughing—and making love.

But he wouldn't change a thing. This thing they had was good, really good.

For as long as it lasted.

Beside him, his phone vibrated, the sudden buzz enough to disturb Ella, and she blinked up at him with her chocolate-coloured eyes. At least her contacts hadn't been stowaways to the mountain.

'I fell asleep,' she said, stating the obvious, and he watched as she registered where she lay. Then smiled as she didn't move an inch, and just looked at him with a contented, half-asleep gaze.

He twisted, careful not to dislodge her, to pick up his phone. Very few people had his mobile phone number, so a message on a Sunday afternoon was unusual.

It was his PA, Kerry:

Check your email.

That was it. It was so unlike Kerry that he opened the email application on his phone with some trepidation—only now realising he hadn't checked it once today. Unheard of…but then, he'd be suitably distracted.

So what was the email? Another request for an interview? Had yet another newspaper felt the need to rehash the old news story of his underprivileged past? Had Georgina sold another 'tell all' story to a magazine that simply rearranged the facts of their relationship into a new saleable product?

Trepidation escalated to foreboding as he registered the number of emails he'd received that day, from everyone from Cynthia, to the VP of Marketing, to a mate he went mountain biking with.

All including at least one of the following words and phrases: *Gossip column, Launch party, Mystery woman…*

He swore, not particularly quietly, and Ella sat up abruptly in surprise. 'What's wrong?'

'Seems I didn't imagine that person on the staircase.'

Ella's eyes widened. *'What?'*

His laptop was closed, but switched on as always, on the coffee table. He flipped it open, and navigated to the Sunday paper's website.

A few moments later he'd located the gossip section and, half expecting a huge photo of he and Ella kissing to be displayed in full technicolour, he breathed out a sigh of relief when that was not what he discovered. Instead, it was simply a short paragraph, halfway down the page:

Spotted! Jake Donner, multimillionaire founder of Armada Software, canoodling with a mystery woman during the launch of Armada's first smart phone on Friday! No word yet on the identity of the lucky lady, but whoever convinced this famously private bachelor to participate in such a public display of affection needs to tell this gossip columnist her secrets. And by the way, faithful readers, have you seen Jake's new look? One word for you: Phwoar!

The almost familiar invasion of his privacy made Jake as tense and angry as ever. But this time, he had nobody but himself to blame.

'How could we have been so stupid?' Ella exclaimed, reading over his shoulder and voicing exactly what he'd been thinking. She immediately straightened, and began to pace the room in long, furious strides.

'It's not so bad,' Jake said, acknowledging the irony that *he*, Mr Obsessed With His Privacy, was the calm one in this situation. 'There's no photo, and I have no doubt they would've named you if they knew it was you.'

Ella had her arms wrapped around herself as she paced. 'But what if they find out? You know what the media's like—desperate to sniff out a story.'

Before he had a chance to reply, she continued, her voice becoming increasingly agitated. 'They've got no *right* to put that in the paper.'

He laughed, a short, hard sound. 'You know as well as I do that whether it's right or wrong makes little difference to the media. Besides—we *were* on a public stairway. You're right, we were stupid to kiss where we did.'

He was angry, but for once this was *his* fault. He'd made a mistake, and now he had to deal with the consequences.

Ella walked stiffly to the window that overlooked the valley. She crossed her arms in front of herself, keeping her back to him.

'This is a disaster,' she said. 'I've worked *so hard...*'

Finally the source of her anguish clicked into place. This had nothing to do with him. To do with them.

It wasn't their relationship—or whatever this was—that she wanted to protect.

It was herself.

The realisation hit him like a low blow to his gut.

'You're worried they're going to find out about Eleanor,' he said, absolutely sure he was right.

Ella turned to face him, the sunlight behind her casting a long, feminine shadow across his floorboards. She nodded, a short, sharp movement.

'Would it really be that big a deal?'

How could this woman who laughed with him, loved with him, care so much about what other people thought? Faceless strangers that didn't matter at all?

She gaped at him as if he'd grown horns.

'You can't be serious, Jake? No one needs to know about Eleanor. It'll ruin everything.'

She said it with such certainty.

'But, Ella—'

'We need a plan,' she said, cutting him off. The soft, sleepy, romantic version of Ella was gone. She was now all in business-like damage control. 'If anyone asks about it, just say it was a one-off thing. You didn't even know my name. The result of a few too many drinks at the launch party or something. Nothing serious.'

His body jerked a little at her easy dismissal of their weekend together. Which was silly—nothing serious suited him just fine.

It was only supposed to be day. That it had stretched to two meant nothing.

He made a weak attempt at humour to cover his confusion. 'I'm a little offended you think that's a plausible story. I generally ask a woman's name before I kiss her.'

'Please do this for me,' she asked. No, pleaded.

And Jake found it impossible to do anything but nod in response to the soft desperation in those words.

He walked over to her, reached out an arm to—what? Draw her close?

He let his arm fall back against his body. 'So what now, Ella?'

She tilted her chin up and met his gaze with guileless eyes. 'Nothing,' she said. 'It's been a really great weekend, but, you know, I should probably get going.'

He opened his mouth to…what? Protest?

Why? He agreed with her. This could never be anything more.

But a disloyal voice in his head disagreed: *It had been so quick. Too short.*

He wasn't even close to getting Ella Cartwright out of his system.

And he was pretty sure he wasn't out of hers.

'I don't want my name in the papers, Jake. You might not agree, but I've got no interest in having my past laid out for all the world to see.'

Her wish to protect the raw elements of her past—the loss of her parents, the bullying, her housing commission upbringing—*that* he could understand. His success had forced his history into the public eye, but Ella hadn't asked for any of this. She didn't deserve to have her pain cut and pasted into a lurid tell-all magazine exposé just because of him.

But the rest, her desperation to hide her past from, not just the media—but from *everyone*. Her friends, her colleagues, her life…

And it wasn't even her past she was hiding—it was Eleanor. She was hiding *herself* from her world.

He might be called the millionaire recluse or whatever, but he never hid who he was.

That Eleanor worked so hard to do exactly that he could never understand.

'I should go,' she said hurriedly, walking past him and towards the stairs to his room before he realised what was happening.

Despite everything, his instinct was to stop her. To ask her to stay...

But how long? A few more hours? Another night?

There was no point.

She'd made up her mind, and so had he.

Only a few minutes later she was back, and he still stood exactly where she'd left him, staring at the view, but to be honest he wouldn't have noticed if a herd of elephants had moved into the valley while he'd waited.

'I'll drive you home,' he said, but she shook her head.

'I don't want to put you out,' she replied, and those simple, tautly polite words really said it all. They weren't friends. They weren't a couple. They weren't even lovers any more.

It was over.

'How about I drop you off at the train, then?'

She nodded.

They drove in silence. When they arrived at the station, she turned to face him. Opened her mouth to speak, only to snap it shut.

Words whirled about in his mind, too, but refused to form into anything remotely intelligible. He was caught between having too much to say and yet nothing at all.

Finally, within seconds of each other, they both spoke.

'As long as we are *very* discreet—'

'If we both agree this is nothing serious—'

The both fell into silence again, but this silence had a luscious tension.

He leant forward, breathing in the scent of her—Ella mixed with the familiar musky scent of his shower gel.

He leant even closer, so his breath brushed against her ear. 'So...'

He smiled when she shivered.

She turned her head, now so close that if either of them moved his lips would brush against hers.

'So...' she murmured, and the corner of her lovely lips kicked upwards.

He closed that insignificant gap, and instantly she curled towards him, her arms snaking up to wrap behind his neck. It wasn't a gentle kiss—rather one tinged with urgency, as if they were both keen to eke out as much as possible from this undefined *thing* they had—for however long it lasted.

After long, long minutes, they finally broke apart.

And Jake put the car in reverse, turned around, and drove them back home.

CHAPTER THIRTEEN

ELLA was absolutely fine with their arrangement.

Fine with the fact she and Jake met up nearly every night after work—or after her Pilates class, or book club or whatever. Always staying in for dinner, of course, to avoid any chance of a repeat appearance in the gossip pages.

He didn't invite her up to the mountains again. Instead they met, in a very cloak-and-dagger fashion, at his apartment in the city. With the media interest in Jake at fever pitch, they never left, or arrived, together. Instead, Ella got to repeatedly experience the unglamorous reality of being dropped off and whisked away from his building via a rather shady back street, courtesy of a trusted Armada driver. This indignity was mostly offset by the exuberant greeting she'd then receive from Albert and Lizzie on arrival—followed by the rather more sophisticated welcome provided by Jake.

Yeah, she'd become quite the fan of Jake's very sexy way of letting her know *exactly* how glad he was to see her.

So they had fun. They chatted, they laughed, and they made love. But they never woke up beside each other—by necessity she was whisked away before dawn. She and Jake could then face the world each day as if the other didn't exist.

She had insisted on this, and Jake had been only too happy to agree. Discretion was of upmost importance to both of them.

So of course she *was* absolutely fine with their arrangement.

Fine, fine, fine, fine, fine.

'Are you okay?' Mandy asked, nudging Ella's champagne glass a little bit closer towards her. 'You look like you need this.'

Ella shook her head, trying to refocus on the here and now. The *here* being the open-air bar beneath Sydney's opera house, and the *now* being a last-minute drink with Mandy she'd organised after Jake had cancelled on her, with only the vaguest of explanations.

Not that she was bothered by that.

'You know,' Mandy said, looking at Ella thoughtfully through a tangle of long blonde fringe, 'I don't think I've ever seen you like this.'

'I'm not *like* anything,' Ella replied. 'I'm fine, honestly.'

That word again. *Fine.*

'Right.' Mandy paused to sip her Blue Curacao cocktail. 'Want to talk about it?'

Yes.

Wait. Where had that come from? No one could know about her and Jake.

No one.

'No,' she said, although it sounded a little unsure. 'Thanks, though,' she added, more briskly.

Mandy sighed, then tilted her head as if assessing her. Automatically, Ella ran her tongue against her teeth and over her lips—did she have a rogue fleck of parsley or something from one of the little bowls of tapas they were sharing?

'Any interesting clients at the moment?' Mandy asked suddenly.

'Nope.'

'You're sure? A friend said she saw you at the Armada Smart Phone launch. With Jake Donner.'

Ella shrugged, although it took all her effort to appear utterly unworried. 'Oh, yeah. I worked with him for a couple of weeks.'

Mandy raised an eyebrow. 'Apparently you both looked *very* friendly on the dance floor. And I've heard rumours about Jake and some 'mystery woman'. Any idea who that might be?'

Her implication was obvious. Others had made the connection, too, and she'd fielded a few calls from journalists in the days following that damn gossip piece. Fortunately, it appeared, her denials had been effective, and she hadn't heard a gossipy whisper since.

'No,' she said, although she hated to lie to Mandy. So she offered a partial truth. 'We just went to school together. That's why we looked friendly.'

Her friend shook her head, then went silent for long seconds.

'You're a funny thing, Ella Cartwright,' Mandy said, quite slowly, as if delivering a statement of fact.

'Pardon me?'

'I hadn't noticed, really, until just now, but I don't really know anything about you, do I?'

Ella laughed. 'What are you talking about? We hang out all the time.'

But Mandy didn't pay her words any attention. 'Like, I read somewhere that Jake Donner's from Perth, right? Three-thousand-odd kilometres away? So you must be, too.'

Reluctantly, Ella nodded.

Mandy smiled, but didn't look particularly happy. 'And I didn't even know that.' She shrugged. 'I thought we were friends.'

'We are!' Ella said, a little shocked. 'We've had heaps of fun together.'

'Exactly. But that's all we ever do. Have fun. You know, it's only been recently we've started hanging out more, just the two of us. I like it.'

It was strange, seeing perfectly gorgeous heiress Mandy Williamson be just slightly vulnerable. Strange, and also more than a little uncomfortable.

As if now Ella would be expected to be vulnerable, too.

And that just wasn't an option.

But, for the first time, Ella felt a twinge of guilt for deliberately basing her friendships on good times and *not* on some deep, emotional connection.

It was her own fault they were having this conversation. Until recently, Mandy had been someone she liked, someone she respected, but someone, like everyone, that she kept at a distance. Really, she'd even considered her closer to an ex-client than truly a friend.

But then something had changed, and she'd found herself reaching out for more to her. Needing more...

Because of Jake.

It was Jake who'd pushed her off balance. Who'd made her life feel less like a perfectly tailored shirt and more like a pair of stockings with ladders running all the way through them. Of course she'd reached out to a friend, of sorts, to try and rearrange her thoughts, her emotions, her confusion back into something she could control.

But it wasn't permanent. It was *temporary.*

Once he was out of her life again, everything would go back to normal.

And Jake Donner would walk out of her life. Of that she had no doubt.

For that reason, she pasted on a smile. 'We *are* friends, Mandy. But trust me, you don't want to hear too much about me. I'm terribly uninteresting.'

She took a casual sip of her champagne and lifted her shoulders as if she didn't have a care in the world.

Mandy's lips thinned. She placed her glass carefully back on the table, slid from her bar stool and then gathered up her handbag where it lay at the base of the tall cocktail table.

'I've got to go, Ella,' she said, not meeting her gaze.

The champagne on her tongue tasted suddenly bitter. Awful. With an effort, she swallowed, the liquid forcing its way down a throat tight with unexpected disappointment.

'That's a shame,' Ella said, with bubbliness as false as Mandy's eyelashes. 'We'll have to catch up again soon, okay?'

Mandy nodded, probably the result of unconscious, conditioned good manners more than anything else. Then she walked away.

Leaving Ella amongst a sea of people in the packed bar, the Sydney city skyline to her left, the harbour bridge lit up be-

fore her, and the dramatic curves of the Opera House towering above her.

Alone.

Jake sat beneath the too-warm lights of the midday show's studio, doing his best to smile, and look attentive and open, while
feeling more than a little ridiculous in the make-up he'd been
told was compulsory.

'Now, Jake, can you tell us what it is about this new Armada
phone that makes it so exciting?' The host, a woman with helmet-
like blonde hair, arranged her plumped-up lips into an encouraging smile as she waited for his answer.

It seemed impossible that the campaign was only three weeks
old. Jake felt as if he'd been smiling, and talking, and smiling,
and schmoozing for months. And months.

But still, he took a deep breath, and, just like the good little face of Armada he was, he obediently launched into an 'on
message' answer to the question. By now he'd done so many
variations of this very same interview he could talk about the
phone in his sleep.

'Well, Gloria, what really makes this phone stand apart is its
operating system...'

And so he went on, doing his best to intersperse geek speak
with more consumer-friendly explanations.

According to the very happy marketing department, he'd
been getting that just about spot on. Early sales of the phone
were well above expectations. Focus groups were indicating a
significant increase in brand recognition.

Basically, he was ticking all the boxes.

And while it was reassuring to know it'd all been worth-
while, it didn't make this particular interview any less mind-
numbingly boring.

'Now, just one more question before we finish. I happened
to stumble across an interesting snippet in last weekend's Sunday paper...'

Jake tensed. It was the question he'd been expecting all week,
just that so far he'd been fortunate enough that his schedule

had been more of the technological variety—an interview for a smart-phone magazine, an appearance at a new technologies conference and the like.

But this was commercial television at its finest, complete with a live studio audience rabid for news of the tabloid variety. Of course she'd been going to ask.

The host recapped the pertinent details, ending with a kissing-sound special effect.

Ah. Classy.

'So tell me, Jake,' she asked conspiratorially, as if they weren't surrounded by hundreds of people and a television crew, 'just who is this lucky lady?'

He and Ella had discussed this. He knew exactly what to say.

Yet the words didn't come, not immediately.

Instead, most unexpectedly, he was reacting as he had at that radio station. No, he didn't have the urge to throttle over-peroxided Gloria. But his body was suddenly constructed of knot after knot of tension.

He didn't even want to say *no comment*. He wanted to end the interview—immediately.

Even though he knew that to do so would be stupid. Even though he knew it would achieve nothing but further scrutiny.

The host was looking positively gleeful at his extended silence. He could hear the murmur of whispered voices in the crowd, and he knew every camera was trained right on him.

What would the average Australian, sitting at home on their couch at noon on a Friday, be able to see in his face?

Could they tell what he was feeling? How hard it was for him to lie?

Lie. Was that what he thought he was about to do?

And if he thought that, what did that mean for him and Ella?

He managed a laugh that sound awfully false to his ears. 'We all make mistakes, don't we, Gloria? It was nothing.'

'So she's not your girlfriend?'

'No,' he said.

'You're sure about that?' she asked. 'You seemed to have a good long think about it.'

'Absolutely,' he said, and now he was back using the inter-view voice he'd cultivated over the past few weeks.

The host chuckled. 'Well, I'm sure that will come as a huge relief to many, many women. Hear that, ladies? Jake Donner is still on the market...'

He barely heard what the host said next, but the next thing he knew he was being ushered from the stage, and plonked down in front of a mirror to have that caked-on gunk removed from his face.

He should be relieved. It was another issue-free interview. One more campaign appearance to cross from his list.

But he felt...

Uncomfortable.

And...guilty.

Why?

He'd done nothing wrong. He'd had no reason to stumble when asked the question. It was what he and Ella had agreed.

Maybe it was just his choice of words. As he couldn't classify the past week as a mistake, whatever Ella might think. Or if it was, it was certainly one he'd be happy to make again and again.

This thing, this arrangement? Fling? Whatever it was, it didn't feel like a mistake. Whenever he saw her, in fact, it felt quite the opposite. It felt right.

With her, he didn't have to pretend. And, to a point, he felt she didn't pretend with him. Although she'd never let her guard down again as every time they'd met she'd been picture perfect with not a strand of hair or a smudge of make-up out of place, complete with those fake green eyes.

He wished she could see that she didn't need all that stuff.

Slowly he registered the direction his thoughts had taken.

This felt right? With Ella?

He firmly pressed down on his mental pause button.

No way. He was *not* going there.

He was not going to start paying attention to the siren call of intimacy. Of relationships. Of *love*.

The very idea triggered an almost suffocating pressure in his chest, and at his throat—an overwhelming sensation that over the years had become so, so familiar.

He couldn't do this.

He needed to cancel tonight. They were meeting at his place in a few hours' time.

No. Not cancel. He needed to see her tonight—and end it.

Yes. That was what he had to do.

Ella reached blindly for the remote, and pressed far harder than was necessary to rid her television, and her apartment, of the echo of Jake's words.

We all make mistakes.

It was nothing.

Too late she realised the midday show had long ago moved to a commercial break, and it was purely her own brain that was insisting on replaying those short, painful little sentences, again and again and again.

Painful?

Why? He'd done nothing more than recite the words she'd fed him.

That she'd *pleaded* for him to say.

On her couch, she drew her knees up to her chin, not caring that she was wearing a designer suit that would not appreciate such unladylike treatment.

She wasn't supposed to care. She was supposed to be *fine*, remember?

But even though it was irrational…

Her heart still ached.

And what that might mean frightened her in ways she couldn't possibly describe.

Ella had just returned from her Pilates class when someone buzzed to be let into her building.

She'd hoped that exercise would provide her with that promised rush of endorphins, and so by now she'd be feeling happy and perky and *normal* again. But no such luck. As she walked to the panel beside her door, she felt just as confused and un-settled as she had since Jake's television interview.

Although, if she was honest, she'd been unsettled for lon-ger than that. Last night she'd found herself wishing she'd done what Mandy had wanted, and what she suspected *she* needed, and poured everything out.

But she wouldn't even know where to start. What was *ev-erything*? How could she possibly put the way Jake made her feel into words? How she feared what they had ending almost as much as she feared what she might soon feel for him? Or maybe already did?

No. It was better that she hadn't talked to Mandy.

Because if she started, she didn't know if she'd ever be able to stop.

She stabbed at the button on the intercom panel. 'Hello?'

'Ella, it's me.'

She was sure, for a moment, her heart ground to a halt.

'Ella? Can I come up?'

She managed to push the buzzer that would let him in, but didn't say a word.

Why was Jake here?

She'd come no closer to figuring that out when she opened the door to let him in.

Before she'd even had a chance to say hello, he reached for her, placing a hand at the small of her back to pull her against him.

He wasn't rough, but he was sure. Her softness moulded to the firm, hard lines of his body. This close to him, any possi-bility of analysing or deconstructing her relationship, such as it was, with him, evaporated. This close to him, she could barely think at all.

'Jake?' she said. 'Is everything okay?'

For an answer, he kissed her, hard, and fast.

'What is this?' he asked as they broke apart, breathless. 'What we're doing?'

She looked up at him. His gaze, usually so steady and so cer-tain, was all over the place. He'd meet her eyes, then flick away.

Look down to her lips for a long moment, then move his gaze away again—over her shoulder, out of the window.

What did he want her to say?

She didn't need more than one guess. He wanted reassurance that this was just fun. It was physical, and that was all.

He didn't want talk of expectations. Of wanting more. Definitely not about love.

Love?

That wasn't a word she'd considered. And wasn't about to.

She liked him? Yes. Too much? Definitely.

But love? No.

She wouldn't make the same mistake twice.

If she was ever tempted, well… She only had the example of her father, and herself, to refer to. She could never allow herself to need someone like that. As her dad had needed her mum. As she'd needed them both—and Jake.

She was never going to suffer the pain of lost love again.

'This is nothing,' she said, repeating what he'd said on the radio. She said it flatly, careful not to betray one skerrick of how she'd felt when she'd heard the words. As if the tiniest of daggers had slid between her ribs, and dangerously close to her heart.

'Nothing?' he repeated.

She nodded. 'It's just something that's good as long as it lasts.'

'And how long will that be?'

Ella knew then, instantly, that she should end it. Right now. Because the answer to that question, the one right on the tip of her tongue, was *for ever*.

And how dumb was that? Jake didn't want that. Couldn't offer that. She didn't want that either.

She didn't.

But saying the words she needed to say to end this, to decide that this was the last time that Jake would hold her in his arms? She just couldn't do it.

'I don't know,' she said, trying to sound cool and relaxed. 'I guess we'll know, right?'

God. She was such a coward. All she was doing was dragging out the inevitable. He was going to hurt her. Again. It was only a matter of time.

He nodded.

Then he kissed her. And as always happened when he did, she forgot about anything else but how good that felt.

They'd fallen asleep.

Ella woke to a looping snippet of a movie's theme song, and she spent a few moments trying to figure out why on earth that might be.

But, slowly, other details began to register. The rise and fall of Jake's chest, only centimetres in front of her eyes. The flickering light throughout her lounge room, courtesy of the patiently waiting DVD menu. The cool air against her bare toes where they poked out from the bottom of the blanket.

How lovely it felt to be lying in Jake's arms.

She had no memory of how they'd come to be sleeping together this way, with Jake's back to the TV, and herself pleasantly squished between the fabric back of her sofa and the solid wall of Jake's body. She was sure it hadn't been a conscious decision, by either her or the man beside her.

She'd watched him, taking advantage of the simple luxury. And it was a rare one—given they'd barely slept that first night together, and he hadn't let himself fall asleep beside her since.

So she saw the exact second he started to stir, and was waiting to meet his gaze when his eyelids slid open.

It was dark in the room, despite the light thrown by the TV. But she could still see *something* in his eyes. Something indefinable.

'Ella,' he said, whisper soft. His hand touched her hip, then travelled ever so slowly downwards to the dip of her waist before flowing back up to her shoulder. Wherever he touched her body burned. Deep inside, she glowed. The whole time, he kept his eyes locked on hers.

His fingers slid along her collarbone, touching bare skin where the scoop-necked T-shirt she wore gaped open. She shivered.

Then he explored upwards, gently brushing against the cords of her neck, outlining the shell of her ear, skimming along her jaw.

She sucked in a breath as he leant in close, but he paused, not quite touching her lips. When he pulled back from her, just a little, her eyes widened.

'Jake?'

The hand that had almost reverently touched her body had curled to cup her cheek, but now he released her, to trace the shape of her lips, the curve of her eyebrows, and then the slender straightness of her nose.

He didn't have to repeat what he'd said the last time he'd done this.

He said he didn't care if her nose had a bump or was straight. If her eyes were green or boring old brown. If her name was Eleanor or Ella.

Before, she'd been quick to react, to lash out at the words she'd assumed were insincere. Throwaway words to make the ugly girl feel better.

But here and now, in the intimacy of darkness, she let herself wonder, just for a heartbeat, that maybe the words were true.

She tried. She did, but it was impossible. She just couldn't believe.

What she *could* believe was that something had changed. Altered.

With this man she'd known for as long as she could remember. With this man who made her laugh, who made her body sing, and who made her sigh when he watched her with *that* look in his eyes. With this brilliantly smart yet more-than-often clueless man who frustrated her with the way he seemed to know her far better than she knew herself.

With this man she'd only just realised, lying here in the almost darkness, that she'd missed so terribly.

With this man she loved.

The realisation didn't even begin to surprise her.

Was it only hours ago she'd been lecturing herself on the dangers of such an emotion?

Of course she'd been right. Wise, even. Her life free of the complications and pain of need, and love and emotion, had served her well for a very long time.

Changing tack here was misguided. Foolish. Reckless.

It was all those things, and yet she was helpless to do anything about it.

It was a cold hard fact. She loved Jake Donner.

Because it was the only thing she could do, she kissed him. And when he kissed her back, the sensation was all-consuming.

They kissed in a way that made their explosive kisses of the past fade by comparison. This was a kiss of heat, and of seduction—but also a kiss that spoke all the words that she could never say.

Then Jake was standing, barely breaking contact with her lips as he scooped her into his arms. He carried her, effortlessly, to her room, where they tumbled, together, onto the softness of the bed.

A tangle of limbs, and a tangle of emotions.

The next morning, Jake woke up early. Just before dawn.

Ella lay, curled against him, her hair fanned out across her pillow and spilling onto his.

One of her hands rested gently on his chest. As he breathed he watched her hand rise and fall, rise and fall, over and over again.

His heart beat against her fingertips, hard and fast. Far harder and faster than made sense for a man who was lying naked in bed with a beautiful woman.

Or maybe it made perfect sense.

Ella shifted, then stretched, her lashes fluttering open.

She smiled as she tilted her chin upwards to look at him. 'Hey,' she said, all sleepy and sexy.

His chest felt tight.

He'd been gutless. He'd come here to end things, but the instant he'd seen her, it had seemed impossible.

So they'd both pretended that this was, just as he'd said, and *she'd* said: *nothing.*

But that lie had been exposed in all its glory that last time they'd made love. He couldn't even begin to describe what that had been, but it certainly wasn't nothing.

He'd thought he could do this with Ella and it wouldn't mean anything. That it wouldn't get complicated.

He'd been wrong.

He needed space.

'Jake?' she asked as he extracted himself from under her with little finesse. He switched on the bedside light, the sudden brightness shockingly stark.

'I'm going to go for a walk,' he said.

'What? Now?'

He squinted at the clock radio on her bedside table. 6.04 a.m.

'I'll go buy the Saturday paper,' he said, as if that explained everything.

He snatched up his jeans and shirt from her bedroom floor, dragging them on in rough, automatic movements.

Ella sat up, tugging the quilt up over her breasts. 'Come back to bed,' she said. 'It's dark outside.'

'It'll be light soon,' he said, not looking at her at all.

The room was silent save the sound of Jake dressing.

'You're running away,' Ella said suddenly. A statement.

'No. I'm getting the paper.'

But he was running. In a way. At least for a while. Maybe longer.

'I like space,' he said. 'Silence.'

He couldn't do this any more. He was uncomfortable. Uneasy. He needed time to think.

Jake looked at Ella once more before heading for the door. That was a mistake.

She watched him with the strangest expression in her eyes.

She was the Ella of the night before, on the couch, who had gazed at him, who had smiled at him, and who had kissed him in a way that had simultaneously touched him—and terrified him. In a way that had him desperate to run away right this minute. But that last night had had him entranced.

'Stay,' she said softly.

But he shook his head. A second later, her gaze turned flat. Neutral.

She straightened her shoulders in a subconscious action that was heartbreakingly familiar.

'Fine,' she said, in a totally different tone from before. Not quietly sexy, but instead bright. Almost cheery. She yawned, then actually grinned. 'Right. I'm going back to sleep. Can you grab a carton of milk while you're out, too?'

Ah. He knew what she was doing. Suffocating that little glimpse of vulnerability with a pasted-on smile and words that were as false as they came.

She was back in her Ella armour.

He didn't let himself think about that. Think about what that meant, what she'd revealed before she'd rebuilt her sparkling façade.

Space. He needed space.

Then he walked out of her room, out of her apartment, and onto the deserted footpath outside her building.

Then he walked. Walked, and walked and walked.

With his mood matching the darkness of the sky.

CHAPTER FOURTEEN

WITH an inoffensive little click, Ella's apartment door shut behind Jake.

Something louder—gunshot loud—would've been more appropriate, given the way her body jolted beneath the layers of sheet and quilt.

Then she was alone, in awful, horrible, absolute silence.

Tears stung her eyes, and she could taste them in her throat, but she was not going to cry.

She swallowed, and stared hard at the ceiling, refusing to let those tears fall.

She wasn't going to cry for Jake again.

Once in a lifetime was enough.

Unfortunately, her heart seemed incapable of similar once-in-a-lifetime rulings. There was no denying it now. It hadn't been her hormones confusing lust with love in the heat of the moment—although she badly wished it were.

She'd fallen for him again.

Ages ago, probably. Maybe when he'd turned up on her doorstep ready to do almost anything to share with her something he thought was special. Or even earlier, when they'd laughed together in the middle of the street.

Maybe she'd never stopped loving him.

She tried to sleep, but it was impossible. In the dark, in the silence, and without Jake, she felt terribly, terribly alone.

So she got up, turned on the radio. Had a shower. Threw out

the discarded pizza boxes from the night before. Checked her email. Cleaned the dishes in her sink. Made the bed.

When she finally ran out of things to do and Jake still wasn't back, she plonked herself on the couch and switched from the radio to Saturday-morning music videos as her silence-filler of choice, and planned what she was going to say when Jake, finally, came back.

He was going to end it. He was walking out there trying to figure out some nice way to break it to her.

At least this time she wouldn't suffer quite the same humiliation. She hadn't told him she loved him.

Not in words, anyway. In thirteen years she'd at least learnt that.

But it was still going to hurt.

It already was.

She jumped as her little apartment filled with the sound of the door buzzer. She leapt to her feet. There was absolutely no point in delaying the inevitable. She needed to treat this like pulling off a Band-Aid. If she was quick, it would be less painful.

Right.

By the time Jake made it to her floor, she'd pulled open her front door and was waiting for him.

The second he stepped inside, she spoke, aiming for pure nonchalance. She could do this. 'Jake, you know how we said last night that we'd know the right time to...'

She kept speaking faster and faster, the words cascading like rapids over rocks, fast and violent. But suddenly the waterfall of words trickled down to nothing.

What Jake held in his hands had as good as wrapped fingers around her throat. She opened her mouth. Closed it again.

Then she blinked. Blinked again. Reached up automatically to push her glasses up her nose before remembering she hadn't worn them in years.

But surely her eyes were playing tricks on her?

Jake held a single page of the newspaper out to her, but she couldn't make herself take it from his hands.

Frozen, glacial, horror overwhelmed her.

She took a step backwards only to smack into her lounge-room wall.

'Ella? It'll be okay…'

Jake reached for her, but she had no interest in his touch. Instead she staggered past him to collapse on an armchair, immediately putting her head between her knees.

This could not be happening.

'Hey,' he said, his voice low and presumably intended to be soothing. It failed. 'I know this is a shock, but if you read the article, it's not that bad—'

Her head snapped up. '*Not that bad?* Jake, it's a full-page article in Sydney's biggest newspaper. And it's about *Eleanor.*'

'It's about you and me,' Jake clarified. 'We weren't quite as discreet as we'd hoped, and someone did some digging. They found out we used to be friends. Found a few old photos.'

'*Found a few old photos?*' she repeated, knowing this was verging on hysterical behaviour but incapable of anything else. Any which way she looked at this, this was a disaster.

Of epic proportions.

'It's actually surprisingly accurate,' Jake said, still frustratingly, ignorantly calm. 'Just the facts. It could be a lot worse. I've had whole articles written about me based on lies.'

He was so unaware.

'Don't you get it, Jake? Accuracy is the problem. I thought I made it clear how hard I've worked to move on from being Eleanor. No one in Sydney knows about her. I've *told* you that. No one knows how sad and pathetic she was.'

'You're doing it again, talking like Eleanor's a separate person.'

'She is,' Ella said, matter of fact. 'Of course she is. Look at me.' She looked down at herself in her skinny jeans, loose singlet and bare feet. 'Well, me dressed properly. With my hair and make-up done. Me at meetings, at parties, at nightclubs. When I was Eleanor I could never have done any of that.'

'Of course you could. You do already. You're still Eleanor, Ella.'

She shook her head, trying to figure out words that could possibly explain. 'Don't pretend you don't remember what it was like for me at high school. When I was just Eleanor, I was invisible.'

No, it'd been worse than that. She'd been seen—noticed—and summarily rejected. Again and again.

She couldn't comprehend becoming that girl again.

What was everyone going to think? Her friends? Her clients?

'I've worked *so* hard,' she said. 'And now it's ruined.'

She looked up when Jake deposited one of her dining chairs directly in front of her, and took a seat, his elbows resting on his thighs as he leant forward.

'You think you've been exposed as a fraud,' he said quietly.

'Because I have,' she said immediately. 'My whole life is built around Ella. Not Eleanor. Eleanor undermines everything I've worked so hard to achieve.'

'You're not, you know. A fraud. It's just like you told me, and you tell your clients. You've become your best self—a confident, more stylish version of Eleanor. But you're still *you*. That's clearer to me every day.'

'I've changed,' she said. 'I'm a different person. I have a life, and friends…'

'Friends that don't know anything about your past though, right?'

Ella didn't like the censure in his tone. What right did he have to criticise her?

She stood up abruptly, then stalked across the room to the window, keeping her back to Jake. 'This is all your fault, you know. You and your stupid hermit tendencies. If you weren't so damned reclusive, no one would give a stuff about your personal life.'

'If you weren't so ridiculously in denial about your past, you wouldn't be in this situation, either.'

He was right behind her, and she spun around to face him. He looked tall, and broad, and frustration edged every muscle in his body.

'And you think living up on that mountain in your turret isn't ridiculous?'

'This conversation isn't about me,' he pointed out.

'But of course it is,' she said. 'Thirteen years ago we were both pretty much the same. Poor. Unpopular. Socially inept. But you took one path with your life, and I took another. Given you seem to think your method is superior to mine, then, yes, I do think this is about you, too.'

'It's far more sensible to just ignore a society that judges so much on the superficial. No one valued me until I had money and fame through my work. I'm not interested in buying into a world that will treat people that way.'

'Ah. So noble of you,' she said, and his eyes narrowed at the mocking lilt to her tone

'And yet here you are, devastated because people will judge you for being more than the sum of the clothes you wear, your hair and your make-up?'

'I've told you before,' she said, her tone getting sharper by the minute. 'Image is everything. My image was everything.'

Jake took a step back, but somehow Ella knew this was no indication of him backing down.

'What are you worried is going to happen?' he asked.

'I'll lose my friends. Clients.'

Everything.

'Why? You can't believe your only value is in your appearance?'

'Why would I believe anything else?' she said.

Jake attempted another angle. 'When you came to Sydney, what did you want?'

She recited the familiar words. 'Confidence. Polish. Success.'

'And you've achieved them all.' He rubbed his forehead. 'I still don't get it, Ella. So what if you've got some dorky photos in the paper? They don't change what you've achieved.'

He was never going to get it. He'd never understand what she stood to lose. If she acknowledged Eleanor, it would inevitably all flood back.

Deep down, that was who she was. She was unpopular, unattractive and clueless. All that social failure and rejection was just waiting—lurking there beneath the surface.

She was a fraud in glossy packaging.

And if she wasn't Ella any more, what did she have?

She was Eleanor. In love with Jake Donner. And he didn't love her back.

She'd come a full, sad, pathetic circle.

'You don't have to be perfect, you know. Everyone has a past. Most of them awkward. Maybe this is a good thing, maybe this will help you let go a little—'

'I think you should go, Jake,' she interrupted, suddenly so incredibly tired. 'It's over.'

'No, Ella, I can't, you're—'

'What are you saying, Jake? It's not over?' Of course she had no doubt of the answer to that question.

'I can't do this, Ella.'

He went to speak again, but she needed to get this out, for him to understand before he walked out of her life for ever.

'You think I'm stupid to care about clothes, and make-up, and the colour of my eyes, because you think it's all fake. You're trying to tell me now that it doesn't matter that I've got my old photos in the paper, but I tell you what, Jake, until I learnt all that stuff, I was alone. Now I'm surrounded by people. By my friends. And you know what? I don't care if I've only got that through all that superficial stuff, as it's a hell of a lot better than not having it at all.'

'But can't you see that it's *you*, not your hair or your clothes that people connect with?'

'So you're telling me that if I got rid of it all, nothing would change?'

He nodded. Bless. He actually believed that.

'You're so much more that what's on the surface, Ella.'

He couldn't be that naïve. 'Such pretty, meaningless words, Jake. Especially coming from someone with his own façade. You've built your own wall between the world and you. And you refuse to let *anyone* past it.'

'Just because I don't like the city and I'm not out night after night doesn't mean I—'

'No, Jake. You've let your screwed-up childhood warp your ideas of love and relationships and trust. So you've switched off your emotions, rather than risking experiencing them yourself. I can't think of a better way to build a barrier between yourself and anyone who dares to get close to you.'

He raised his eyebrows. 'I thought you didn't need anyone, Ella. That you didn't need love.'

She shook her head. 'That's what I've been telling myself. Unfortunately I'm beginning to realise that I can't control my heart as well as my clothes, or my hair, or my make-up. I might not want love, but sometimes it just…happens.'

'What do you mean?' Jake said, his voice urgent.

'Oh, you already know, Jake. It's why you ran away this morning. You don't need me to put it into words.'

Jake looked as if he didn't know where to go. What to do.

She waited and waited for him to speak, but he remained totally silent.

'How about we put your theory to the test, Jake? That it's me, that it's *Eleanor* apparently that people want?' She straightened her shoulders, then held her arms out wide. 'Here. Here's me. Ella slash Eleanor. Twenty-nine years old. I like books, movies, dancing and socialising. But here's a little secret: I'm kind of plain without my make-up. My hair is this really boring pale shade of brown. Dark blonde, maybe, if you're being kind. My eyes aren't really green. I have to work *really* hard to maintain this weight. I reckon my body would be way happier with an extra ten kilos. I'm painfully shy. I needed to teach myself to socialise. I study fashion or I'd never get it right. Do you…' she swallowed, her throat as dry as sandpaper '…want me?'

Neither of them said anything for long, long moments. Long enough that she realised the TV was still blaring, blasting some totally inappropriately upbeat dance track into the silence that hung between them.

'You're not being fair, Ella. You and I have nothing to do with *this*.' He shook the newspaper he still held roughly. 'You and I won't work because we both want different things. You want the city and I need the mountains. You want buzz while I want quiet.' He paused. 'You want love, and I can't give it to you.'

'Well,' she said, after the longest time. 'I guess that answers my question, then.'

'No, *no*, it doesn't. You never stopped being Eleanor, just that now you have a fancy name. You're perfect as you are—you always have been. You need to trust me. Believe that.'

But not perfect enough for Jake. Not perfect enough for him to even consider love.

'I think you should go now,' she said.

This time he didn't protest.

Ella stared straight out of her window, her body stiff as a board, as she listened to him walk out of her apartment, and then, with that damn soft click of her front door behind him— out of her life.

Only then did she start to crumple.

CHAPTER FIFTEEN

HOURS later, Ella sat in her lounge room, alone with the newspaper article. She'd laid it on her coffee table, but wasn't capable of reading it just yet. Instead, she sat cross-legged on the couch, with an oversized bowl of ice cream, untouched, on her lap. Occasionally she eyed the article warily, almost as if it would leap up and scream:

FRAUD!

Long ago she'd switched off the television. And she hadn't bothered to turn on her iPod. Somehow silence seemed more appropriate.

Her phone was switched to silent, too, and left well away in her bedroom. It had been buzzing, earlier. Text messages, missed calls. But she had no intention of answering them. Not today, anyway.

Because she knew what the calls would be about, of course. Probably some journalists, possibly some shocked friends, although she figured that was less likely.

A lot of people would think she'd lied to them. They wouldn't want anything to do with her any more, and she really couldn't blame them.

She'd lost everything today.

Her shiny, perfect, spectacular life.

And, her love.

Was it crazy that it was the loss of Jake that hurt the most? He'd been back in her life for two minutes, while she'd taken nearly a decade to build her world here in Sydney.

Three weeks ago her business, her social life, her clothes—had meant *everything* to her. If anyone had asked, she would've said her life was complete. She had everything she'd always wanted.

Confident. Polished. Successful.

She'd had it all.

But even without the damned newspaper article, without this ruination of all she'd worked so hard to achieve, would that have still been enough for her?

No, she realised, it wouldn't have.

Even without the unveiling of Eleanor the dork and the outcast, the shy girl, the plain girl, the invisible girl, the rejected girl...

Even without all that, her life wouldn't have been the same after today.

Because Jake had ruined it, too.

He'd made the so-called completeness of her life a lie.

Every single thing she'd called Jake on—the barriers, the walls, the self-protection at the cost of real emotional connection—she was guilty of them all herself.

She was no better than Jake up on the mountain in his turret.

She was in her own. A rather trendy inner-city turret, complete with fabulous wardrobe—but a turret, nonetheless.

And now she needed more.

Ella dumped the ice cream in the sink, and walked slowly to her room.

Perched on the edge of her bed, she picked up her phone.

22 missed calls.

47 new messages.

Ella scrolled through them all, her stomach doing nervous somersaults. Searching, searching, searching...

Even though she'd told herself not to hope—and that she didn't want to hear from him anyway!—her heart got just that little bit heavier when Jake's name didn't appear.

Except, that wasn't who she was really looking for.

It was Mandy. But there wasn't a missed call from her. Or a message. Not one.

Her shoulders slumped, and she stretched out her arm to deposit the phone back on her beside table.

At least she had her butterscotch ice cream for company...

No.

She wasn't going to do this any more. It was time for her to stop following her stupid, self-imposed rules, to finally, after far too long, let people back into her life. To let people *in*. To share her emotions.

To risk rejection. To risk loss.

To *live*.

So, with fingers that shook, and the tears she'd cried for Jake still damp on her cheeks, she dialled Mandy.

And held her breath while it rang.

The final week of the *Jake Donner* campaign was nuts. It had been planned that way. He had a conference presentation, an appearance at a trade fair and one final newspaper interview.

Of course, now he had the added scrutiny of the tabloids, all desperately ravenous for the latest salacious piece of gossip. This time, he had no intention of toning down his infamous glare. Let the papers write what they wanted, call him what they wanted, but he was not going to smile and pose for them. His and Ella's relationship was off limits. Full stop.

Amongst all this distraction, he still had his actual job to do, too. And so, each day was long, and full—a blur of activity.

About the only thing that wasn't a blur were the rare occasions he allowed his mind to wander. Rare, because it seemed determined to wander in only one direction: Ella.

Then his thoughts were crystal clear. All he would see was that image of her, wrapped in her multicoloured quilt, her shoulders bare, her hair all over the place.

Absolutely beautiful, and absolutely perfect.

Asking him to come back to bed. Asking him to stay.

It didn't matter how hard he tried, that image wouldn't go away.

And it would appear at the most inopportune moments. Like

right now, on a Sunday afternoon, where finally he had a day free. There was no need to go into the office, as he'd had to yesterday. He didn't even have one email to write. Or code to review.

Today was a day he had completely to himself.

So he sat on his balcony, comfy on the battered leather armchair he regularly dragged outside for this purpose, a beer in his hand, alone but for the view.

It was the tail end of winter. Spring was trying really, really hard to impose itself, offering up a decent attempt at a sunny day. His dogs had stretched themselves out at his feet, their bellies exposed to the half-hearted rays.

This was his definition of bliss.

He stretched his legs out long, relaxed into the chair, and closed his eyes behind his sunglasses.

Bliss.

Bliss.

BLISS.

Yes. It was.

He determinedly kept his eyes closed, and concentrated on relaxing. Waiting for the familiar shift—the moment his brain let go of the minutiae of the everyday and truly let go. Finally, it did.

For about five minutes.

This is all very nice and everything, but…

It does get kind of boring after a while…

Ella. Her words.

He'd disagreed with her that day. He'd been unable to imagine ever agreeing with her. He loved it out here, loved the mountains, loved the silence.

But today, it wasn't the same.

Today, he wasn't just alone.

Today, for the first time, he was *lonely.*

His eyes popped open.

What?

He stood, and strode over to the balcony rail and gripped it, hard. Hard enough that it hurt his palms. Hard enough to force himself to think straight.

This was his sanctuary. Ella called it a turret, but that hadn't bothered him, not really. It suited him, having this place that was his, and certainly no one else's. His space. His place.

He needed it. This escape.

But now it was ruined. He knew it, bone deep.

It was never going to be the same. Ella had changed this place.

Together they'd created memories here that touched everything.

He couldn't be in this house without thinking of her. He couldn't walk on his own property without thinking of her.

Jake stared out to the mountains. What now?

Sell up? Buy another place? Another escape?

Immediately he knew that wouldn't work. Immediately he recognised what doing so would actually be: It would be him running away. Again.

He'd run away from his past, years ago, when he'd left Perth. He'd told himself he'd been leaving his dysfunctional family and generations of inherited failure—and that had been part of it. He hadn't been able to shoulder the circus that was his mother any longer. Her roller-coaster emotions, her absurdly declared love for him and the zero substance that supported it.

But even back then he'd been running away from how he felt about Ella. From the depth of her emotions. From her need for him.

He'd closed himself off, frightened by emotions he didn't know how to handle. That he didn't know if he could actually believe.

But what had leaving achieved?

Guilt.

Now he knew why he'd never called Ella. Never reached out for her again.

She'd been living in the same city as him for *eight years* and he'd had no idea. What a waste, what an awful, terrible waste…

All because of his guilt. Guilt that he couldn't handle what she'd needed from him. Couldn't handle the volume and breadth of her grief for her mum, or her love for him.

Was that why he'd closed off his emotions? Because if he allowed someone else to love him, he might fail them too?

As he'd failed his mum when he'd left. As he'd failed Ella.

But now—he was about to do it again.

But this time it was worse. This wasn't some teenage crush he was throwing away.

This was love.

He loved her.

He had to repeat it a few times in his head, then, finally, aloud, before the reality sank in. Really sank in.

And he didn't feel suffocated, or panicked or pressured.

He felt...*right*.

It was an immoveable, inescapable truth that he was in love with Ella.

And he needed to fix things.

Fast.

He called her, immediately, but she didn't answer.

She wouldn't, he realised. Nor would she open her door to him.

He needed a Plan B.

A week later, Ella and Mandy relaxed in wicker chairs at Bathers' Pavilion on Balmoral Beach. Sun streamed through the floor-to-ceiling windows, and an early morning breeze worked its way determinedly through the louvres. Before them sat their half-finished mountains of blueberry pancakes and, beyond that, glorious views of Middle Harbour all the way to the Heads.

'So, brown eyes today, then, Ella?' Mandy asked, meeting Ella's gaze over the rim of her cappuccino.

Ella nodded. 'I felt like a change,' she said, although that wasn't entirely it.

Of all her memories of Jake—one seemed particularly reluctant to be dislodged.

Oh, who was she kidding? Her subconscious would overflow

with Jake—images, words, sensations—the instant she let her guard down even the littlest bit.

But one memory leapt forward more often than the others.

She was lying on a quilted blanket, surrounded by the noisy silence of the mountains. Above her was Jake, looking at her the way no one ever had before. And her eyes had been brown.

Was it stupid to hold onto that memory and to throw away her green contacts so she was reminded of Jake whenever she looked in the mirror?

Yes, undoubtedly.

But, she wanted to hold onto that moment. That moment when she'd felt free, and when anything had seemed possible. Where, fleetingly, she'd felt truly beautiful.

'It'll get easier,' Mandy said.

Ella gave a little shake of her head. 'I know.'

But it was going to take a heck of a long time. At least another thirteen years, Ella reckoned.

'We should go out dancing next weekend, maybe? To take your mind off things?'

Ella couldn't quite believe what had happened since that newspaper article had been printed two weeks ago.

She hadn't got it all wrong—she'd shocked a lot of people. And hurt people too, people she'd known for years who'd only just found out how little they truly knew about her.

But from amongst the huge number of people she'd called her friends, a smaller number had risen to the surface. Real friends, people who'd ached for her, for her public humiliation, and, more importantly, for the sadness from her past, and the recent pain because of Jake.

Eleanor had been revealed, and yet Ella had been left far from alone.

Picture Perfect had even had a record week of new clients. Who would've guessed?

Jake had. He'd known.

He'd been right. She'd never stopped being Eleanor. Just back in Fremantle she'd been too scared to step out of the stereotype she'd been so firmly assigned in high school, even long after she'd left. She'd built up so many stupid walls to protect herself that even in Sydney, surrounded by people, she'd still been truly alone.

There were no walls now. It still scared her a little, but there would be no going back.

'Dancing would be fabulous!' she said to Mandy, and they spent long minutes discussing their options.

Mandy had been the biggest surprise. It had taken a heartfelt apology—and that was all—for Mandy to turn up at her doorstep, with chocolate chip cookies to supplement her woe-is-me ice cream. Ella seriously didn't know how she would've survived the past two weeks without her.

Or how she'd survived these past thirteen years without a friend like that.

'Oh, look,' Mandy said, nodding towards a couple who passed by the front of the café. 'You're still a semi celebrity.'

Ella didn't even cringe any more. After two weeks of people asking, 'Hey, aren't you that girl from the paper?' she'd really had to get over it.

So she smiled at the couple who waved at her. And then the group of teenage girls who'd for some reason pointed at her excitedly.

So, yeah, it wasn't so bad, and, besides, the number of people who'd felt the need to confide their similarly tragic high-school lives to her had been kind of wonderful. It was yet another reminder that she was definitely not alone.

All that was missing was Jake.

But if she tried, really hard, she only missed him a couple of hundred times each day.

Out on the beach, yet more people noticed her. This time, a grey-haired couple, who smiled and waved in unison.

'I thought it would've died down by now,' she said to Mandy. 'Surely I'm old news?'

Mandy shrugged. 'Apparently not.'

Hmm.

As she slowly drank her coffee a crowd began to gather along the beach. It was cool, not really a day for any but the most dedicated of swimmers. And besides, the crowd were mostly in jeans, not bathers.

'I wonder what's going on?'

Mandy just shrugged. A newspaper had been folded on the edge of their table, and her friend reached for it, and settled in to read as Ella observed the carryings-on.

The crowd continued to grow, and eventually Ella noticed a couple of television network cameras.

She found herself peering out to the ocean, looking for something, anything, that could be causing so much fuss.

'Mandy, you've got to look at this. It's bizarre.'

'Hmm,' her friend said, patently uninterested. 'Hey, I'm reading a really fascinating article. Do you want to have a look?'

She shook her head. Honestly, whatever was happening out on the beach was far more exciting.

'Ella, I really think you should read this,' Mandy said, much more insistently.

Ella glanced at her friend. 'Give me the highlights,' she said, then looked back out to the harbour. The crowd seemed to have congregated around something, about halfway between the shore and the boardwalk.

'It'll make more sense if you read it yourself.'

As Mandy was as good as waving the paper in her face, she grabbed it with one hand, letting it fall open on her lap on the page of this, oh, so important article.

But she kept her eyes on the beach.

'Ella,' Mandy said, 'please read the article.' A pause. 'Now.'

'What's so interesting that I must read it right…?'

Her voice petered off into nothing as the huge block capitals that took up a full page of the paper bounced off her brain.

That *could not* be right.

Ella Cartwright—meet me at Balmoral Beach. 9 a.m. I have something I want to ask you. Jake Donner.

Ella realised her hands were shaking.

'Honey?' Mandy asked. 'Are you okay?'

She looked up, and Mandy stood beside her. She nodded.

'Then you'd better get your butt down to that beach. You're running late.'

With legs as weak as jelly, Ella managed to stand. Around her, every single person in the café was watching her. Smiling.

'You were in on this?' she asked Mandy, trying to make head or tail of it all.

'Uh-huh. But you're on your own now.' She gave her a gentle shove. 'Go on.'

Somehow, she managed to put one foot in front of the other, and was then out of the café, onto the promenade, and kicking off her leather sandals, stepping onto the beach.

The sand was surprisingly warm beneath her toes, and her shoes dangled from her fingers, bumping in a regular rhythm against the fabric of her jeans.

As she approached the dense crowd of people began to disperse, backing away just a little, but she still felt all their eyes on her.

And then, from amongst it all, stepped Jake.

In bare feet, faded jeans, and a white shirt, rolled up to his elbows. As he walked towards her, he just smiled. He didn't seem to notice all the people, or the cameras that hovered only metres away. He had eyes only for her.

'Hey,' he said, a metre away from her.

'Hey,' she answered softly. It had been only two weeks since she'd last seen him, but still she drank him in. She'd missed him. 'Um, Jake, what's going on?'

'I wanted to say I'm sorry. For being such an idiot.'

'Okay,' she said. Then couldn't resist adding, 'I'm sorry you're an idiot, too.'

He laughed, shocked, at first, and then real and genuine. Ella grinned right back at him.

He reached for her, and her shoes dropped to the sand when he took her hands in his.

'I love you,' he said.

She closed her eyes, not quite believing what she was hearing. It had been so, so long that she'd hoped. That she'd waited.

He gripped her fingers tight. 'Ella?'

As if she'd ever let him go now.

She opened her eyes, tilting her head up to look at him. The morning sun made her eyes squint, but she was well beyond caring what she looked like.

'I love you too.'

And he let out a breath he must have been holding. It made her smile, as if there'd ever—*ever*—been any doubt.

'Well, that's good news. This would've been rather embarrassing otherwise.'

'You mean the advert in the paper, and the media?'

'That too. You wouldn't answer my calls.'

'This seems a rather extreme solution,' she pointed out.

'And I wanted you to be sure I meant it. That I wouldn't change my mind. And the funny thing was, for the first time in my life, I *wanted* everyone to know something about me. I want everyone to know how much I love you, and how lucky I am to have you.'

Tears prickled, and she swallowed, desperately, then realised it didn't matter. She had nothing to hide. Who cared if she messed up her mascara on Balmoral Beach on national TV?

She was in love with Jake Donner, and he loved her. That was all that mattered.

She could cry happy tears as much as she wanted.

'What was the other thing,' she asked, 'that you said would be embarrassing?'

'Oh,' he said, with the most wicked of grins and a dangerous sparkle to his eyes. 'That would be this.'

And he dropped to one knee, and, miraculously, a velvet box appeared from his pocket. He snapped it open, and the sun made the diamond glitter in a million remarkable directions.

'Ella, will you marry me?'

And because her legs had lost all ability to hold her upright, she fell to her knees before him.

And with tears in her eyes, she said *yes*.

Then the ring was on her finger, and she was in his arms. Around them, the crowd cheered, and cameras flashed, but all she had eyes for was Jake.

'You're so beautiful, Ella.'

And even with mascara running down her cheeks and sand in her hair, she believed it.

EPILOGUE

LATE on a January afternoon, and without a film crew in sight, Ella walked towards the shade of a scribbly gum.

The summer sun warmed her shoulders and the softest of breezes ruffled the fine silk of her ivory dress. In her hands she gripped her posy of tulips tightly—not because she was nervous, but to remind herself this was real.

There was no aisle. No white carpet. No chairs, even.

There *was* Mandy, gorgeous and smiling as always; and a friend of Jake's, Paul, beside her, with Albert and Lizzie sitting neatly at their feet.

Ella had discovered that Jake had managed to accumulate a friend or two over the years. All were either massive computer nerds like Jake—or massive fans of mountain-related adventure-type activities, also like Jake. Consequently, she liked them all.

She thought she'd surprised Jake, too. Their arrangement, with Monday to Friday in the city—with Jake popping up to their mountain home during the day whenever he felt like it—then the weekends always up here, worked well. But while he'd accompanied her to the occasional dinner out with friends, and even one charity ball, reluctantly at first, slowly he'd loosened up. No, he was far from a social butterfly. But he was trying, for her, and he'd even admitted that socialising with her friends wasn't completely miserable. She thought she'd caught him even having a good time—once or twice.

Ella's satin ballet flats were silent on grass that hadn't yet baked to a summer gold, and it was suddenly so still she was sure she could hear the rapid beating of her heart.

Ahead of her stood the celebrant, directly in front of the towering tree's trunk, and to the right of her, in a shirt the same colour as Ella's dress—but wearing no tie, of course—was Jake.

He caught her gaze as she approached, and held it, tightly.

When she finally reached him, she tilted her head up, drinking in the sharp angles and strong planes of his face, dappled in light filtered by gum leaves. She wanted to remember this moment, to capture it for ever in her memories.

'You're beautiful,' he whispered. And Ella smiled.

Of course she hadn't stopped wearing make-up—she loved the stuff—but she'd toned it down, just a little. She didn't need to hide behind it any more.

'You're not wearing jeans,' she said. Instead he looked particularly gorgeous in black tailored trousers.

He grinned. 'Anything for you, Ella.'

Anything, it seemed, was right. Recently, and only because she'd asked him, they'd started visiting his mother's nursing home. Diana didn't hate Jake. Even with her mind permanently damaged by drugs, it was obvious the opposite was true. No, things weren't okay between them, and maybe they never would be, but it was a start. This morning, they'd had breakfast together. And as they'd told her about the wedding, Diana had smiled.

Jake had noticed, too. Ella might have even detected the slightest sheen to his eyes.

One of the dogs—Albert—barked, and Ella laughed, smiling up into Jake's gorgeous blue gaze. Seemed the crowd was getting restless.

Ella twisted to hand her bouquet to Mandy, then turned back to Jake as he gripped her hands in his.

'Can you hear that?' he said.

She didn't need to ask what he meant.

So she listened to the silence. To the rustling leaves above them, to the shuffling noises the dogs made as they couldn't help but fidget. And then beyond, to the distant call of a magpie. The creak and groan of surrounding bushland packed full of ancient trees. To the noisy silence of the mountains.

Silence that didn't scare her any more.

She loved music, and movement and fun, but when it was just her she no longer needed noise to block out the truth.

The truth that she was alone.

Because she wasn't alone. Not any more.

She had friends, real friends, who loved her for who she was, not because she always said the right thing, or behaved the right way, or had amazing shoes.

And she had Jake. And he had her.

She nodded, smiling.

'It's perfect, isn't it?'

Then, ignoring the grumblings of the celebrant, who muttered something about doing things in the correct order...

Jake kissed her.

And Ella kissed him back.

* * * * *

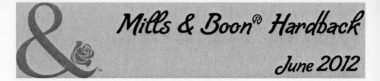

Mills & Boon® Hardback

June 2012

ROMANCE

A Secret Disgrace	Penny Jordan
The Dark Side of Desire	Julia James
The Forbidden Ferrara	Sarah Morgan
The Truth Behind his Touch	Cathy Williams
Enemies at the Altar	Melanie Milburne
A World She Doesn't Belong To	Natasha Tate
In Defiance of Duty	Caitlin Crews
In the Italian's Sights	Helen Brooks
Dare She Kiss & Tell?	Aimee Carson
Waking Up In The Wrong Bed	Natalie Anderson
Plain Jane in the Spotlight	Lucy Gordon
Battle for the Soldier's Heart	Cara Colter
It Started with a Crush...	Melissa McClone
The Navy Seal's Bride	Soraya Lane
My Greek Island Fling	Nina Harrington
A Girl Less Ordinary	Leah Ashton
Sydney Harbour Hospital: Bella's Wishlist	Emily Forbes
Celebrity in Braxton Falls	Judy Campbell

HISTORICAL

The Duchess Hunt	Elizabeth Beacon
Marriage of Mercy	Carla Kelly
Chained to the Barbarian	Carol Townend
My Fair Concubine	Jeannie Lin

MEDICAL

Doctor's Mile-High Fling	Tina Beckett
Hers For One Night Only?	Carol Marinelli
Unlocking the Surgeon's Heart	Jessica Matthews
Marriage Miracle in Swallowbrook	Abigail Gordon

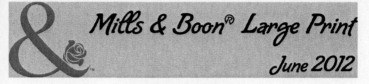

Mills & Boon® Large Print
June 2012

ROMANCE

An Offer She Can't Refuse	Emma Darcy
An Indecent Proposition	Carol Marinelli
A Night of Living Dangerously	Jennie Lucas
A Devilishly Dark Deal	Maggie Cox
The Cop, the Puppy and Me	Cara Colter
Back in the Soldier's Arms	Soraya Lane
Miss Prim and the Billionaire	Lucy Gordon
Dancing with Danger	Fiona Harper

HISTORICAL

The Disappearing Duchess	Anne Herries
Improper Miss Darling	Gail Whitiker
Beauty and the Scarred Hero	Emily May
Butterfly Swords	Jeannie Lin

MEDICAL

New Doc in Town	Meredith Webber
Orphan Under the Christmas Tree	Meredith Webber
The Night Before Christmas	Alison Roberts
Once a Good Girl...	Wendy S. Marcus
Surgeon in a Wedding Dress	Sue MacKay
The Boy Who Made Them Love Again	Scarlet Wilson

0512 GEN STD LP

Mills & Boon® Hardback

July 2012

ROMANCE

The Secrets She Carried	Lynne Graham
To Love, Honour and Betray	Jennie Lucas
Heart of a Desert Warrior	Lucy Monroe
Unnoticed and Untouched	Lynn Raye Harris
A Royal World Apart	Maisey Yates
Distracted by her Virtue	Maggie Cox
The Count's Prize	Christina Hollis
The Tarnished Jewel of Jazaar	Susanna Carr
Keeping Her Up All Night	Anna Cleary
The Rules of Engagement	Ally Blake
Argentinian in the Outback	Margaret Way
The Sheriff's Doorstep Baby	Teresa Carpenter
The Sheikh's Jewel	Melissa James
The Rebel Rancher	Donna Alward
Always the Best Man	Fiona Harper
How the Playboy Got Serious	Shirley Jump
Sydney Harbour Hospital: Marco's Temptation	Fiona McArthur
Dr Tall, Dark...and Dangerous?	Lynne Marshall

MEDICAL

The Legendary Playboy Surgeon	Alison Roberts
Falling for Her Impossible Boss	Alison Roberts
Letting Go With Dr Rodriguez	Fiona Lowe
Waking Up With His Runaway Bride	Louisa George

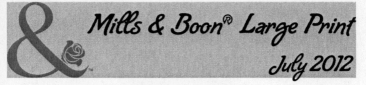

ROMANCE

Roccanti's Marriage Revenge	Lynne Graham
The Devil and Miss Jones	Kate Walker
Sheikh Without a Heart	Sandra Marton
Savas's Wildcat	Anne McAllister
A Bride for the Island Prince	Rebecca Winters
The Nanny and the Boss's Twins	Barbara McMahon
Once a Cowboy...	Patricia Thayer
When Chocolate Is Not Enough...	Nina Harrington

HISTORICAL

The Mysterious Lord Marlowe	Anne Herries
Marrying the Royal Marine	Carla Kelly
A Most Unladylike Adventure	Elizabeth Beacon
Seduced by Her Highland Warrior	Michelle Willingham

MEDICAL

The Boss She Can't Resist	Lucy Clark
Heart Surgeon, Hero...Husband?	Susan Carlisle
Dr Langley: Protector or Playboy?	Joanna Neil
Daredevil and Dr Kate	Leah Martyn
Spring Proposal in Swallowbrook	Abigail Gordon
Doctor's Guide to Dating in the Jungle	Tina Beckett

0612 GEN STD LP

WEB/M&B/RTL3 HB

Discover Pure Reading Pleasure with

**Visit the Mills & Boon website for all
the latest in romance**

Buy all the latest releases, backlist and eBooks

Join our community and chat to authors and other readers

Win with our fantastic online competitions

Tell us what you think by signing up to our reader panel

Find out more about our authors and their books

Free online reads from your favourite authors

Sign up for our free monthly eNewsletter

Rate and review books with our star system

www.millsandboon.co.uk

 Follow us at twitter.com/millsandboonuk

 Become a fan at facebook.com/romancehq